COLONY THREE MARS

A SCIENCE FICTION THRILLER

GERALD M. KILBY

D1607981

OUTER PLANET
MEDIA

For notifications on promotions and updates for upcoming books, please join my Readers Group at www.geraldmkilby.com.

You will also find a link to download my techno-thriller REACTION and the follow-up novella EXTRACTION for FREE.

CONTENTS

1. Secret   1
2. Clone   6
3. Council   14
4. Embrace   22
5. Xaing Zu   30
6. AsterX   38
7. Search   47
8. Fire   55
9. COM   66
10. VanHoff   76
11. Subterranean   87
12. Sanctum   97
13. Battle   105
14. Control   111
15. Rock   118
16. Taikonaut Down   128
17. Happening Again   139
18. Chaos   155
19. Jing Tzu   169
20. Dome Five   179
21. Run   191
22. AsterX Land   197
23. While You Were Asleep   206
24. Pandemic   217
25. Ultimatum   227
26. UN   237
27. A New Flag   243
28. Earth   250

Also by Gerald M. Kilby   267
About the Author   269

1

SECRET

D r. Jann Malbec delicately removed the cover on the petri dish inside the biolab's hermetically sealed isolation chamber. She could now see the profusion of bacterial blooms that radiated out across the surface of the agar gel. This was the last living sample of the bacteria that had caused so much death and destruction to the original colony and the later ISA mission.

Yet, for those lucky enough to be immune to its devastating psychotic dementia, it bestowed a biological reinvigoration and rejuvenation. It was a two-faced Janus. It could be both a beginning and an end. On the one hand, it was the very elixir of life. On the other, it was insanity and death.

Fortunately, it posed no threat to the current colony population, as they had all evolved, one way or another, to be immune to its darker attributes. But there were those, currently en route to Mars, that would not be so lucky should they be exposed to it—even though this was the very thing that they sought. One of these missions was already imminent, with others not far behind—all of them hell bent on acquiring this duplicitous mutation.

Jann removed her hand from the joystick controlling the mechanical manipulator within the sealed chamber. She flexed her fingers for a moment, then reached up to the control panel above the unit and flicked open the protective cover on a switch marked *IRRADIATE*. Her finger hovered over the exposed red button—pressing this would send a stream of accelerated electrons directly through the sample, killing all bacteria within and eradicating it forever. She hesitated.

IN THE AFTERMATH of the upheavals that had traumatized Colony Two, Jann realized, that if they were to survive, she would need to have a better understanding of the complex, genetically engineered, biology of the colony's ecosystem. This technology was, after all, the very reason that a human outpost on Mars could ever hope to function. But much of this knowhow was lost in the mayhem wrought by the events of the revolt, specifically the destruction of the Colony Two labs. So, Jann set about building a new research facility in the hope of regaining this lost knowledge. To this end, the medlab in Colony One had been repurposed and extended. New modules were added, and much of the lab equipment that was salvageable had been moved here from Colony Two. It was during this period of rebuilding that she realized the cave where Nills and Gizmo had hid out, during the first wave of infection by the bacteria, was still there, and that only she and the eccentric droid knew of its existence. So she decided to keep it that way, and had sworn the robot to secrecy. Although, quite what that meant for a droid was hard to know. That said, it did seem to be very attached to her and followed her around everywhere. Nills tried to explain its behavior to her many times.

It learns. That's how it's programmed. And like most intelligent beings it learns from experience, by doing things. The more data it has to work with the more it will change and modify its behavior. It has spent a long time with you, Jann. And Gizmo has also saved your ass more than once. So, it has moved you up its hierarchy of priorities. You have become important to it. Basically, it likes you, you are its friend.

Jann also realized, that when they had purged the Colony One environment of the malignant bacteria, they had neglected to consider this hidden space. It was sealed off and environmentally isolated from the main facility. But, if the bacteria still existed down there then it would pose a fundamental threat to any new arrivals. So, shortly after the medlab's reconstruction as a research facility, she and the droid secretly entered the cave and went on the hunt—and it didn't take her long to find it. But rather than eradicate it she took a sample for investigation, isolated in this sealed enclosure and then purged the cave environment. This was now the only living sample in existence.

Since then, she had spent long hours down here, testing, probing, exploring the bacteria. All the time hoping to gain some better understanding of its extraordinary properties. But time was running out. Missions were already on their way to Mars. New people coming—all seeking this very biology.

She could give it to them. Let them have it. It could spare the colony from the pressure to reveal its secrets. If the bacteria were here, then why not just hand it over? But could they be trusted with it? Not be tempted to return it to Earth where it had the potential to cause havoc on a truly global scale? No, it was simply too dangerous. It must be eradicated for good. *Do it!* She commanded herself to press the button—but still she hesitated.

A LIGHT BLINKED on her comms earpiece lying on the workbench beside her. Jann sighed, removed her finger from the button and picked up the comms unit.

"Yes?"

"Jann, where are you? I've been trying to find you for, like, half an hour."

"I'm... eh... doing something. What is it?"

"Operations just picked up a craft entering Mars orbit."

"So soon?"

"Yes, they're here. Nills has called for an emergency council meeting over at Colony Two. He's on his way here to pick you up."

"OK. Tell him I'll meet him in the common room in twenty."

"Will do."

Jann pulled the comms unit out of her ear and put it in her pocket. She looked in at the sample again for a moment as her hand reached for the button on the control panel. She hesitated again, then finally flicked the protective cover closed. She grabbed the joystick and manipulated the cover back on the petri dish, and returned it to its compartment. It would live for another while longer. Maybe after the council meeting she could bring herself to eradicate it—once and for all.

2

CLONE

The clone known as Nills Langthorp exited the main airlock of Colony Two into a bright Martian morning and looked out across the vast expanse of the Jezero Crater. A flat, unbroken landscape stretched before him all the way to the horizon, around three and a half kilometers distant. Out there, far beyond his field of vision, lay Colony One, where Dr. Jann Malbec had chosen to set up home. He had hoped she would stay with him, here in Colony Two, but she had been adamant in her desire to establish a new research facility. Since most of the labs had been destroyed in Colony Two, they had moved all that was salvageable to a new home in the now extended medlab of Colony One.

Gizmo had also gone with her. Nills missed the company of the little droid, missed its eccentric ways and quirky turn of phrase. But it had formed a strong attachment to Dr. Malbec, and seemed to want to be in her orbit all the time. He didn't mind, really. In fact he was glad that the robot was with her, keeping an eye on her, keeping her safe.

Nevertheless, Nills had started building a second *Gizmo* some time back. But he simply could not spare the components needed for its construction. Things were becoming scarce, some would even argue critical. Yes, they had food a plenty, and air and water. But it was the electronics that kept all the control systems functioning, and those they could not fabricate. So as components failed, less critical systems would be scavenged for parts.

This was a situation made worse by the destruction of the labs during the upheavals surrounding the ousting of Dr. Vanji. And it was further exacerbated by a disaster in the resource processing sector some time later. That catastrophe had nearly tipped the viability of the colony over the edge. A hydrogen leak in the lower cavern led to a devastating explosion. Twenty-six colonists died, including all of the Hybrids, except for Xenon—he was now the last of his species. And, as if that wasn't bad enough, most of the machinery used to fabricate basic components was also destroyed.

In the aftermath of this fiasco, the council had argued that the resources of the two colonies should be consolidated into one, it would give them a better chance of survival. But in the end it was felt that retaining both locations would provide them with a better defense against potential subjugation by any of the new forces now heading their way from Earth.

So, Gizmo II was parked as a half-built project and Nills' mind turned to finding a way in which the two facilities could be more efficiently managed and maintained. The big problem was distance, they were over thirty kilometers apart, too far to EVA on foot. So the only way to go from one to the other was by rover, and that could take up to two hours, particularly with a full load on board. So for some time Nills bent his mind to the conundrum of effecting a speedier and more efficient, cross crater, transit. But he also had his own, more selfish, motivation for solving this problem. If he wanted to spend more time with Jann, then he was going to have to come up with a better transport solution. One that could take minutes rather than hours to cross the crater.

The solution, of course, was flight. But not winged flight, as the Martian atmosphere was too thin to make this practical. Nills also ruled out an airship type design for similar reasons. His idea—one which he'd had for some time—was to repurpose one of the landers the original colonists arrived in. Since they used retro-thrusters to effect a landing on the surface, they all came with methlox engines, tanks and a control system for stabilization.

However, it would need a considerable amount of re-engineering to transform it into a true flying machine—one that could traverse the crater. Since it only had the ability to move up or down, not sideways to any significant degree, he would need to add on a forward thruster, as well as lateral and rotational control. The fuel tanks were also too small, affording only a few minutes of burn time. So his first task was to dramatically reduce the weight by stripping it of everything that wasn't directly required for flight, including the outer shell. Since he could operate it while wearing an EVA suit, there was no need to have it enclosed. By the time he was finished it had been reduced down to a bare chassis, just enough to support the four retro-thrusters, tanks and a rudimentary pilot seat of Nills' own construction. The landing gear was permanently extended and the entire contraption looked like some experimental craft from the mind of a 50's NASA engineer. It was nicknamed *the flying bed* or simply *the bed*, for short.

Fortunately, the retro-thrusters were not powerful enough to reach Martian escape velocity, so Nills had no fear of accidentally sending himself into orbit with it. But they were more than sufficient to lift the entire craft off the surface and then some—that took care of going up. For forward motion, Nills added a simple gas powered thruster on the stern of the craft. One of the advantages of a thin atmosphere was very little friction so this unit did not need to be that powerful to get a decent amount of momentum going, and once moving, it pretty much kept on going. He also added lateral thrusters to port and starboard to give him rotational control.

It used methlox—methane and liquid oxygen, as the

propellant, and they still possessed the infrastructure to manufacture plenty of this, in both facilities. So Nills only needed to add enough additional tanks to travel the distance between the two colonies. After each trip it would be refueled and made ready for the return.

From Nills' perspective, it was a thing of beauty. However, it was a view not necessarily shared by Jann, who, while she appreciated the speed at which it could traverse the crater, was not as convinced as Nills was of its mechanical integrity.

Nills walked over to where the bed now sat, its spindly structure silhouetted against the Martian sky, like some giant metal arachnid warming itself up with the rise of the morning sun. He clambered up the superstructure onto the wide, flat platform that served as the passenger area and sat in the pilot's seat. He flicked on the power and pre-ignition check routines started to scroll down a central screen. It would take a few minutes for this process to complete so, as he waited, Nills looked up at the sky above him. Somewhere overhead a Chinese mission, Xaing Zu Industries, had just entered orbit. They would spend the next few sols slowing the craft down by using their main engines and the atmosphere as a braking system, going lower and lower as they slowed, until they had burned off enough energy to enter a stable orbit and prepare for landing.

. . .

FOR A LONG TIME NOW, the colonists had known this would happen, new missions, and new people arriving—all anxious to investigate the strange and exotic world of the colony. But he had mixed feelings about this intrusion, as did the other colonists. On the one hand these new missions would bring badly needed supplies and components that could not be manufactured in situ. And these supplies could ultimately make the difference between survival or death. Not that it was a quick death that faced the colony, but a slow death by a thousand cuts as each component failure would stress the life support a little further each time, until finally, it could no longer sustain its dependents. So Nills had welcomed these new missions, he was, on balance, looking forward to them.

However, Jann was not of the same opinion. In fact, she had an almost visceral paranoia as to the intentions of these new arrivals. It was not a view that Nills subscribed to, although he was not so naive to assume, for one minute, that their motives were truly honorable. No, he knew damn well what they were after—the so-called Janus bacteria. But, since it no longer existed, then what was the problem?

His ruminations were broken by a message flashing on the control screen. *Ready!* It had run through all the checks, time to lift off. Nills settled himself deeper in the pilot's seat, strapped himself in and hit the ignition button. He could feel the vibrations of the pumps kicking in up through his spinal column. It increased in intensity until the control screen flashed *Ready to rock!*

On either side of the pilot's seat, mounted onto the rudimentary armrests, were two simple joysticks. One on the left was simply up/down. This was really the business end of the machine. It was also the moment that Nills loved the most, so he hesitated slightly so as to savor the moment, then he gently pushed the joystick forward.

A massive cloud of sand billowed up and around the craft, completely obscuring his view. The vibrations increased dramatically and, if he had not been strapped in, he would have been bounced off the platform. The dust cloud thickened as he nudged the joystick further, delivering more propellant to the engines. So dense was the dust cloud, that he was never quite sure when he was airborne until the craft exited out through the top of the plume.

He was now fifteen meters or so up from the surface and still rising. When he reached around thirty, he throttled back to hover the craft at this altitude and took a moment to survey the area. It was a clear morning and he now had a commanding view across the Jezero Crater. He nudged the joystick on his right side to rotate the craft in the direction of Colony One, then pushed forward on the same stick. The machine moved off, slowly at first, but all the time picking up speed as it flew over the crater's surface. It would take him less than fifteen minutes to make the trip.

His heart gladdened at the thought of being with Jann again. They had been apart for quite a while, as she spent most of her time holed up in the medlab of Colony One, while he saw to the engineering and maintenance demands of Colony Two. He looked skyward again, as if to catch a glimpse of what was to come. For better or for worse, things were about to change. A new era was now unfolding, one where the humanity of the colony, and all those who called it home, would be truly tested.

3

COUNCIL

After Nills had picked her up, the trip back across the crater for Jann had been uneventful. That is to say, the bed didn't blow up en route. She even began to enjoy the ride, as some moments were truly exhilarating. And it was in those moments that Jann felt more alive than she had for a very long time. Perhaps she had spent too many hours cooped up in her lab, staring down the barrel of a microscope, so to speak. All the time looking inward—seldom outward.

Now though, she was glad in a way that the first of the new missions had finally made it into orbit. At least it gave her an excuse to leave her darkened room and engage with the world, with Nills—she had missed him too. But before any intimacy could pass between them there was a council meeting to undertake. One that required her full attention, because what was decided now could dictate their very survival as a self-governing human colony.

THE POST REVOLUTION colonists had initially established a kind of governance by general consensus, where everybody's voice was heard. This had the advantage of minimizing arguments and fostering an inclusive and harmonious environment. In a sense, it kept everybody in the loop. But as time passed, and decisions on strategy and resource allocation became more important, a new council of sorts began to manifest itself. First to rise to prominence were those who had the knowledge and expertise in the functioning of various sectors of the colony infrastructure: biotech, agriculture, engineering, medical, communications, et cetera. Then there were those that the colonists simply held in high regard, such as Dr. Malbec. The Hybrid, Xenon, was also one such. He was viewed by all as a considered thinker, never rash, one who carefully analyzed the various options and possible outcomes. So, when a final decision needed to be made on some tricky issue, it was generally he they would turn to.

THEY HAD NOW GATHERED in the same council chamber, overlooking the vast central cavern in Colony Two, that the original council of Dr. Vanji had occupied. But this council was markedly different. For one, all were welcome regardless of perceived status in the colony. Secondly, there really was no official hierarchy, save for Xenon sitting at the head of the long stone table. He had taken to donning a dark robe for these sessions, like a Victorian judge. He sat now, as mediator and final arbiter—should that be needed.

In the center of the table, a 3D rendering of the planet Mars rotated, and around this, the current estimated orbital position of the Chinese Xaing Zu Industries spacecraft. Holburn, who knew most about these things, hence his elevation to the role of systems tech, was currently explaining the orbital mechanics that the Chinese crew was undertaking.

"They have to execute several elliptical orbits, using both their main engine and the atmosphere to help slow them down." They all watched as the spacecraft's planetary transit was drawn out in ever decreasing ellipses.

"It will be a few more sols before they're in a position to contemplate landing."

"So, how long is *a few more sols*?" Anika pitched in with the question.

"They estimate three sols to reach optimal orbit. Another one for systems checks and prep."

"Four sols," she replied, and left the words to hang in the air.

The council were all silent for a moment. Their collective gaze fixed on the slowly rotating orb.

"And how long before COM gets here?" It was Jann

who finally broke this moment of communal contemplation.

Holburn consulted a tablet he was holding. "Around fourteen."

"COM are the people we need to worry about the most. Now that they've won the court case to regain ownership of the Colony, all they have to do is set foot in either facility, and it all reverts to them." Anika made a wide sweeping gesture with her hands. "Including everything that's ever been developed here."

Her fears focused on the fact that the Colony One Mars consortium had taken the International Space Agency through the Court of Arbitration to regain ownership of the Colony. And they had won. But there was one caveat, they physically needed to set foot inside either of the facilities before it would all legally revert to them.

"And what happens then? Where does that leave us? Are we all just products of COM's bioengineering division? I mean, will COM own us—physically?"

"That's why we should keep these bastards out. I'm not going to end up as a lab rat." It was a voice from the crowd of colonists that had packed themselves in to the council chamber and taken up standing positions around the walls.

"What choice do we really have? We can't survive, long-term, without critical component supplies from Earth. And once they land, how long could we realistically keep them all out, even if we wanted to?" Nills gestured at the mass of colonists.

"We have no choice but to let this play out." Jann's voice was calm and measured. "I for one, have no love of COM. After all, it was me who prevented Dr. Vanji from leaving, and I also scuppered their original plan. So they'll have it in for me, first and foremost. But there's no point in hiding from it. Nills is right, we have no future in isolation, we'll all end up dead anyway."

Before anyone else could reply, Xenon rose, extended his arms slightly, palms facing out, and spoke.

"It seems, on balance, we have no choice. We must embrace this challenge and try as best we can to assimilate the newcomers. Only then do we have a future."

There was another moment's contemplation by the ad-hoc colony council while they all considered the words spoken by the Hybrid.

"However, that doesn't mean we should make it easy for them," he finally said before sitting down.

Jann now took up the baton again. "Our immediate issue is how best to prepare for the imminent arrival of Xaing Zu Industries. And let's face it, their intentions are clear, they're after the exact same thing as COM. Acquire the genetic knowledge that extends human lifespan and return to Earth with the prize—and achieve this before COM land and reclaim ownership of the facility."

Holburn deactivated the 3D holograph of the planet and sat down. "And what if they don't?"

"Don't what? Find what they're looking for or leave when COM arrive?" said Anika.

"Both, I suppose." He gave a vague shrug.

"The knowledge that they, and COM, seek resides in all of us, it's now part of our DNA. How they plan to divine its properties is not clear. But my fear is that it will involve invasive examination on... selected subjects."

"I'm not going to be a goddamn lab rat," came a voice from the assembled mass of colonists.

Jann raised her hand to silence the outburst. "Even with this, the likelihood of Xaing Zu discovering anything substantive in the time they have available is minimal."

"Meaning they will not be inclined to depart when COM arrive," said Holburn.

"Precisely. So at that point I would envision a face-off between the two parties." Jann replied.

"And therein lies our opportunity," said Nills. "If we can pit one against the other, then..." He made a gesture. "Divide and conquer, as they say."

Again there was a moment's contemplation by the council before Xenon leaned forward and spoke.

"It would seem then, that this is the point where outcomes become uncertain, and thus open to considered manipulation for our benefit." The council all nodded at this summation of the situation.

"So, what do we know of their respective numbers and resources?" Anika pitched her question at Holburn.

He stood up, tapped an icon on his tablet and a 3D rendering of the Chinese landing craft materialized in the center of the long table. "There are eight crew," he began, "generally referred to as *taikonauts*. The commander is Jing Tzu. A highly regarded individual. Two are flight and systems, two are scientists, presumably geneticists. That leaves three that are, well, probably military."

"Weapons?" said Anika

"Unknown. But we should assume they're packing something. Also, and this is curious, they have no transport with them. So they'll be relying on us to move them between facilities."

"Why do you think that is?" Said Anika.

"My guess is that they'll have full fuel tanks, ready to take off again at a moment's notice. So they're trimming as much weight as they can elsewhere. Not having a rover would be a considerable saving."

"And COM?"

Holburn tapped a few more icons on his tablet and the Chinese craft was replaced by the COM lander. It was enormous by comparison, and there was an almost audible moment of awe from around the table when it rendered.

"As you can see, this is a much larger mission. Twelve crew. We have little information on who or what they are bringing with them. But it's safe to assume, judging by the size of the craft, they've brought everything and the kitchen sink."

"Weapons, rovers?" said Anika.

Holburn shrugged. "I would guess, all of the above."

"Okay," said Jann. "Let's focus on Xaing Zu first. The plan is to meet at the landing site and bring them all to Colony One. That's where the research lab is, that's where they want to start."

"Then we should put on a show of force. We'll bring both rovers and the bed, and have some of us visibly armed, just to let them know we won't be a pushover," said Nills.

"I will endeavor to be as open and transparent with them as possible regarding access to the research lab. Let them see that the knowledge they seek no longer exists. Maybe then they'll be satisfied."

"And if not?"

"Then there is still a population of around twenty-five over there, it won't be that easy for them to try and coerce us."

"Maybe for Xaing Zu, but COM will be a different matter."

"True, but there's not much we can do at the moment. We'll just have to wait and see what transpires. Then seize our opportunity, if one should present itself."

"And if it doesn't?" said Anika

Xenon once again rose and spoke. "If such a moment escapes us, then we fail. And if that is the case, then so be it."

4

EMBRACE

J ann sat in the dim light of the balcony, looking out across the expanse of the main Colony Two cavern. Here and there she could glimpse the night shift going about the business of maintenance, their presence evidenced only by the sweep of a torchlight. The ceiling illumination was many hours into its nocturnal cycle, painting the cavern roof with the illusion of stars. She felt a cool breeze across her face from the array of large air recyclers overhead. It felt like a summer's night back on Earth.

"Can't sleep?" Nills' voice drifted out from within the darkened room.

Jann turned her head, trying to penetrate the inner gloom to where she and Nills had been sleeping.

"No, my mind is like a racetrack, it won't let me sleep."

She heard a rustle of sheets and Nills materialized from the dim interior and sat down opposite her on the balcony. He was naked save for a sheet gathered around his waist.

"Want to talk about it?"

Jann looked back across the cavern. "I wonder if we're doing the right thing."

"Letting these guys in?"

"Yeah. Maybe the others are right. We should batten down the hatches and throw boiling oil over them at the gates."

"And how long would that go on for? We agreed the best way forward is to face it head on."

"I know... and you're right, but I just have a bad feeling about it all."

"Well, there's nothing we can do. We don't have what they're looking for so we're going to have to convince them of that one way or the other."

Jann looked over at Nills and studied him for a while. He was silhouetted against the dim light of the cavern, his face obscured save for his bright smile and a faint glint from his eyes.

"Actually, Nills, that's not entirely true."

Nills froze for a moment and Jann could sense his mind was coming to terms with the implications of what she just said.

"Go on," he finally managed.

Jann shifted in her seat, and pulled the sheet around her.

"I went looking for it, in the cave under the medlab in Colony One, the place where I first met you and Gizmo."

"You mean my Alpha."

"Yes, sorry... I didn't mean to..."

"It's okay, I shouldn't have said that... go on."

"Anyway, that was months ago, when we were extending the research facilities."

"And you found it."

"Yes. I isolated a test sample and then purged the cave."

Nills leaned forward. "When were you going to tell me this? Who else knows?"

"Just Gizmo. I was planning to kill it before they got here. I didn't want to burden you with it."

Nills sighed. "Do you still have it?"

"Yes. I was about to irradiate it this morning, before the meeting, but..."

"But what?"

Jann took a moment before replying, then sat forward. "If it's what they want, what they've come here for, then we could simply hand it over, be done with it. It could spare the colony a world of grief."

"And what if they take it back to Earth?"

Jann sighed and sat back again. "Therein lies the dilemma. The irony is if we deny them this then we are doing it for the good of Earth, not Mars, not for us."

Nills thought about this for some time, scratching his chin in a slow absent-minded manner. "Tell no one else," he finally said. "Keep it between us. We've time yet to decide. Maybe it's good... you know, to have an ace in the hole."

They sat in silence for a while before Nills finally spoke.

"Do you ever miss Earth? I mean, it is your home."

"I'm not sure if I know where home is anymore, Nills."

"I'd like to think it's here, Jann. But I know, in my heart, you will want to go back to Earth at some point."

Jann hesitated. "I don't know. There's nothing there for me anymore. My father's dead now and... well, I don't have any other family alive."

"You don't talk about him much, what was he like?"

"He was like any alcoholic, tormented by his demons. But don't get me wrong, he wasn't a bad man. My mother died when I was still a baby. So my father was left to his grief, to the demands of a small farm and to the needs of an infant. It must have been hard."

"Well, from where I'm sitting, he did a good job." Nills smiled.

"It came at a cost, Nills. If I were to sum up his legacy, it's that he instilled in me an almost primal need to run away and hide. And I've come to realize it's probably what defines me. Run and hide, that's all I ever do."

"You're being too hard on yourself, there's more to you than that."

"I grew up on a rural farm, no family, few friends, just myself and my father. Every now and then, when things got too much, he would drink himself into a rage. All the anger, the grief, the frustration would come out in a torrent of violence. Not directed at me, thankfully, but at anything that wasn't nailed down in the house, and some things that were. So, at those times, I would run and hide. Out into the fields to my secret place. I would stay out all night sometimes, staring up at the night sky and wish some alien spacecraft would beam me up and take me on an adventure through the stars. Then, in the morning I would go back. My father would be crashed out on the sofa, or sometimes he would make it to his bed. When he woke up later, he would say nothing, just clean up the mess and be extra nice to me for a few days."

"That must have been scary, for a kid."

"In a way, it's what gave me a love of nature, of biology. My friends were the plants and the animals, and the stars were my dreams." Jann shrugged. "Ahh... I'm getting soppy. I'm sure you're not really interested in hearing about my screwed up childhood."

Nills didn't reply and remained quiet for a time. Finally he shifted in his seat, leaned in closer to Jann and, in a low voice, said. "The family of Nills Langthorp has tried to contact me."

Jann felt a wave of emotion wash over her and she gathered him up in her arms and held him tight. She had always feared this might happen. In truth, she knew it was only a matter of time.

THE COLONY HAD, for some time, adopted a policy of open and transparent communications with the public back on Earth. It had been envisaged as a first-line defense strategy—open themselves up to the world, be accessible and get the people on their side. It helped that Rachel and Xenon were masters at picking the right stories to focus on. The message was controlled, managed and massaged to present the colony, and its colonists, as people you could relate to. They no longer referred to the inhabitants as clones or Betas or Hybrids. They were all simply colonists. The stories were about everyday life in the colony: the trials and tribulations, the ups and downs, the hope and fears. In reality, it was a kind of propaganda.

They broadcast as much as they could over X-band so anyone on Earth with a big enough dish could receive it. This resulted in a number of enthusiastic amateurs relaying all this information via the Internet out to the broader world. By now there were thousands of media channels back on Earth dedicated to dissecting and discussing everything that the Colony transmitted.

Recently, they had been putting out more and more stories about their fears for the colony with the arrival of Xaing Zu Industries, COM, and other planned missions. As a strategy, it worked. People started to question the motives of these corporations, and how they would treat the colonists. So the propaganda war that they now waged mattered. If communications stopped when COM arrived then at least Earth would know that something was not right. How much all of this effort helped in the fight for the colonists to keep control was debatable. In reality it probably didn't matter to the likes of COM one way or the other. They were going to do whatever they wanted and the colonists were powerless to stop them.

But this openness also had some unexpected repercussions. Now that they were open for all to communicate with, the families of original colonists, who they assumed were dead, found that clones existed of their loved ones. Identical in every way to the person they had lost. It raised hitherto unknown emotional and ethical issues for both parties. This communication had to be handled very delicately. Some embraced it, some retreated from it, and some on Earth simply reviled it as being the devil's work, advocating that the entire colony on Mars should be razed to the ground, with everybody in it.

JANN DETACHED herself from Nills and looked at him. "What are you going to do?"

"I don't know. To be honest, I'm a little confused. I mean, I'm not who they think I am. I'm not here to satisfy someone's morbid curiosity."

"You don't have to engage if you don't want to, Nills."

"I know, but... I have memories of them... I really don't know who I am."

Jann moved closer again and held his hand in hers. "For what it's worth, I know who you are. Someone I'm very glad I found."

Nills gave a wide grin. "Now, you *are* getting soppy." He stood up. "Come on, let's try and get some sleep. There's nothing to gain from dwelling on things that have no clear answer. We're here now, so we may as well get on with it."

"You go, I'm going to sit here for a while longer."

He kissed her on the forehead. "Okay, but don't try and work it all out tonight. There's much we don't know yet. Too many uncertainties lie ahead."

5

XAING ZU

Over the next few sols, as they counted down to the arrival of the Chinese expedition, messages began to flow back and forth between the colony and the orbiting craft as arrangements were being made for the landing. Much was already known to the colonists about the history and scale of Xaing Zu Industries. They were a global industrial conglomerate, with interests in space exploration, biotech, mining and more. They had a long-standing helium 3 lunar extraction operation, and also controlled over ninety percent of the global stockpile of many rare-earth resources. Their decision to land near Colony One had been made long before they had lifted off from Earth. And all communication, hitherto, had been polite and efficient, if somewhat clandestine. They gave nothing away about their mission, other than on a need to know basis.

. . .

JANN, Nills and Xenon, along with a few other colonists that constituted the reception party, were in full EVA suits standing out on the planet's surface, well back from the proposed landing site. They had assembled there around an hour ago, and were now all craning their necks to try and spot the telltale streak in the sky that would be the Chinese Mars Descent Vehicle. It should be currently ploughing its way through the upper atmosphere, hurtling towards the surface. All going well, it would land in a few minutes.

"There." Xenon pointed over across the horizon.

They all watched as the speck in the distance grew in size and formed into the recognizable shape of a Mars lander. Finally, its descent slowed as retro-thrusters kicked in, then it was lost in an enormous cloud of dust and sand. They had landed successfully. The first craft to do so since the ill-fated ISA mission. The one that brought Dr. Jann Malbec to this place, many Earth years ago.

"Okay, let's saddle up and go say hello," said Nills. They clambered onboard one of the colony rovers and Jann took the controls. She started up the machine, and headed in the direction of the slowly dissipating dust cloud. As she drew closer, Jann could see just how big it was, maybe three times the size of the now destroyed ISA lander.

"That's a sizable bit of machinery," she said to no one in particular.

"Well there are eight of them. And fully fueled to lift

off again in a hurry," said Nills.

"They're not taking any chances, are they?" she said, as she slowed the rover down.

"Would you? To be fair, they don't know what to expect on the ground. We could turn out to be a ravenous horde of cannibals," said Nills.

Jann pulled up around twenty meters from the base of the craft. A thin cloud of dust still shrouded the enormous lander, giving it a ghostly aura. On her left she could see the second colony rover, driven by Anika, pull up close by. On Jann's right another enormous plume of dust kicked up from the planet's surface as Xenon brought the flying bed in to land. They were all in position. Nothing to do now but wait.

"THEY'RE TAKING THEIR TIME. No sign of any activity." Nills began to fiddle with the comms unit on the rover. "Gizmo, are you sure this is the correct frequency for two-way with the lander?"

"Are you seriously asking me that question?" The robot had made its own way out from Colony One to meet up with the reception party, at Jann's request. She felt safer having it around.

"Wait... look."

On the side of the gleaming white craft a hatch cracked open. It was low and wide, and pushed out from the main structure as it gently rose upward revealing a low, wide gap. From this, a platform extended slowly, giving the impression of a balcony on the side of the craft. From within the shadows of the ship six taikonauts stepped out. They wore gleaming white EVA suits, all identical. The platform slowly started to descend.

"I have to admit that's pretty slick. I feel like we're being visited by a technologically superior race," said Nills. "Okay, well it's time to get our game faces on, let's go"

They clambered out on to the surface and stood for a while watching the taikonauts slowly descend. One waved at them. They all waved back. Jann wondered what they must look like to these clean sleek spacefarers. A band of rag-tag colonists, with their battered and dirty EVA suits, and strange space-trash transport. Like a Mad Max on Mars, probably.

Gizmo moved up beside Jann. "If I am not mistaken, and let us face it, I never am—they have brought a robot with them."

"Where? I just see six crew and some equipment on the platform."

Before Gizmo had time to answer, the elevator came to a rest on the surface, a small plume of dust kicking up from its base. The taikonauts stepped off and waited, while what looked like a stack of equipment unfolded itself and perambulated out on the dusty Martian soil. It was a quadruped, about waist high, with a small head that seemed to be scanning all around it.

"I see it," Jann said as she watched the machine advance.

"It is scanning us, multiple spectrum analysis. Hmmm... that is interesting."

"What is?"

"It just said hello to me. Its name is Yutu, which means *jade rabbit* in Mandarin."

"I don't know which is the most surprising, the fact that they have a robot with them or the fact that you know Mandarin."

"I have been studying many of the Chinese dialects, of which there are hundreds, in anticipation of this very event."

"I'm switching to broadcast, Gizmo." Jann tapped her wrist pad to change comms frequencies. In preparing for this they had agreed a common VHF channel to use for communications. It was old school but worked just as well on Mars as it did on Earth. Jann looked over at Nills and nodded. The three of them then walked forward to greet the new arrivals. Gizmo followed behind.

"Welcome to Mars," said Jann.

One of the taikonauts waved. "It is an honor to be here. I am Jing Tzu, commander of the Xaing Zu Industries Mars Exploration Mission, and on behalf of our crew we are humbled to be among you on this momentous day."

Nills stepped forward and extended a hand. "I am Nills Langthorp, pleased to meet you." They shook hands. "And this is Dr. Jann Malbec."

"Ah... Dr. Malbec, we have heard so much about you."

Jann simply shook his hand and nodded. The other taikonauts all hung back and said nothing. Jann noticed that they were distracted by the Martian vista, preferring instead to look all around them rather than focus on the colonists. Yet she felt they had a distinctly military air about them.

The robot, Yutu, sat down on its hind legs, like a big cat, beside the commander. Gizmo was studying it intently, its head twitching as it probed. Yutu looked to be doing the same thing. It reminded Jann of two dogs meeting for the first time. She half expected them to start sniffing each others' butts.

"We can assist carrying your equipment and supplies on to the transport," Nills waved an arm behind him at the two colony rovers and the bed.

"Thank you for your kindness and consideration but we can manage it on our own."

"No, I insist, it's no problem." Nills nodded to the other colonists and they moved forward to help carry the boxes that were now being emptied onto the surface by the crew. This provoked an immediate reaction from the Chinese. They stood together, blocking the way, one held his hand out signaling for them to stop. The broadcast channel broke into a chorus of excited Mandarin chatter. The colonists halted, and looked over at Nills. Jing Tzu turned back to his crew and jabbered in a sharp authoritative manner. This seemed to calm them all down a bit. He returned to face Nills and the colonists with his hands in the air. "Please accept my apologies, we are all a bit anxious from our journey."

Nills nodded. "That's okay, we'll leave you to carry your own equipment, then."

Jing Tzu bowed. "You are most gracious." He returned to his crew and started gesticulating wildly.

Jann flipped her comms to private. "They're a bit jumpy."

"Understandable," said Nills.

"I wonder what's in the boxes that's so important?"

"Who knows? Maybe it's a year's supply of fine whiskey."

"How do we know they're not full of weapons?"

"We don't."

"Well, we can't risk them bringing in concealed weapons." Jann stepped forward towards Jing Tzu, and flipped her comms to broadcast. "Commander, it was agreed that we cannot allow weapons inside the colony. Once we are there you will allow us to conduct a thorough and complete search of your equipment. Is this acceptable to you?"

Jing Tzu nodded. "Yes of course, we understand."

"Very well. When you're ready we can move out."

Jing Tzu turned back to his crew and looked to be explaining this new procedure to them. It was met with confusion by the others, like they were trying to decide something. Then they removed two boxes from the stack and returned them to the craft. Jann and the other colonists watched all this unfold. When the cart was repacked, Jing Tzu signaled that they were ready. Nills climbed up to the cockpit of the bed and fired it up. He waved to Jann.

"I'll see you all back there." With that, the thrusters fired up a great plume of dust as it rose into the air and flew off across the crater. Jann stood beside Xenon as they watched the Chinese board the waiting rovers.

She turned to Xenon, her back to the rovers. "Did you see them putting those boxes back in the craft?"

"Yes, I did."

"Weapons. And lots of them."

"It would seem so."

Gizmo whizzed by them, with the Chinese robot Yutu following close behind. Jann was not sure what they were doing, racing? Seeing how fast each other could go? Or was Gizmo being chased? It was hard to know what went on in the mind of a robot.

Yutu broke away and joined the Chinese contingent. Gizmo looped around and headed over to where Jann and Xenon were.

"I see you've found a new friend. Gizmo."

"That machine is not my friend, Jann. It is a feebleminded conglomeration of spare parts. I do not like that robot."

6

ASTERX

Xaing Zu Industries and the Colony One Mars consortium were not the only corporations planning missions to the red planet. But of the others, only one stood any real hope of achieving such an enormous undertaking, and that was the asteroid mining company, AsterX. It was headed up by the charismatic tech billionaire, Lane Zebos, who was currently looking out a window in the giant rotating torus of the AsterX space station. From this vantage point, he could see the central axle of the mining facility stretch out above him, and the dark brooding form of the kilometer wide asteroid that was grafted onto its terminus. All across the surface of this primeval rock was dotted robotic mining installations, like spiky metallic carbuncles.

Some years ago, his company had conceived of an audacious plan to capture a near-earth asteroid (NEA) and park it in orbit around the planet where it could then be mined for all it was worth—which turned out to be a considerable amount, as it had a core rich in platinum.

But that was then, and soon Lane Zebos was looking around for the next challenge. His searches kept returning him to that great swath of rubble that spread itself out between the orbits of Mars and Jupiter—the asteroid belt. But this would be a mammoth undertaking, a bridge too far, even for an asteroid mining company with the skill and experience of AsterX. It was only when the colony on Mars popped back onto everyone's radar, revealing itself to be very much alive, that a mission strategy began to formulate in his mind. One which might just be possible. And the first leg of that strategy was get to the red planet.

LANE LOOKED up at the central truss of the mining station. Attached to it, and now coming into full view as the torus rotated, was the AsterX Mars transit craft, ready to embark. All they needed was the official mission authorization from the State Department, so that they would be in compliance with the Outer Space Treaty. Lane glanced at his watch, *this is cutting it very fine*, he thought. To take his mind off the waiting, he pulled a cigar canister from the top pocket of his shirt, unscrewed the cap, and slid a thick Cuban Cohiba out into the palm of his hand. But he didn't light it. That would be later.

Instead he brought it up to his nose and inhaled the deep redolent aroma.

"You're not planning on lighting that up?"

Lane looked over at Chuck Goldswater, his chief technical officer, and gave him a wink. He slid the fat smoke back into its metal sarcophagus and returned it to his top pocket.

"Well now, that depends."

"You think the scrubbers will handle the heart attack they're going to get if you kick that thing off in here?"

Lane smiled. "When I actually get to light this bad boy up then I couldn't give a damn about what the systems think of air quality." He raised an extended finger at Chuck. "That's one of the great things about being the boss. I get to do what I like."

Chuck laughed. "Ha, maybe so, but it's still a filthy habit."

"And you're a philistine, with no understanding of the deep pleasures of smoking tobacco. Granted, it's a dying art form, practiced now only by the true connoisseur." He made a kind of a flourish with his hand.

"You're full of shit, Lane."

"Anyway, you know I only partake when something truly worthy merits it." Lane sat back down into a well upholstered white leather seat, and swung it around a few degrees to get a better view of the universe gently rotating outside.

"You think we'll get the oversight we need?" Chuck slumped back into his chair.

"We'll know soon enough."

"It's ridiculously antiquated when you think about it, the Outer Space Treaty and the need for private operators to get some government rubber stamp before we can do any mission."

"Yeah, I know. It's frustrating. As far as I can see, it just gives them an opportunity to meddle and look important."

"Life was easier before COM went and sued the ISA. Back then this would just have been a formality. Now everybody is running scared."

"Yeah, Mars has turned into a political and legal minefield."

Chuck looked at his watch. "What's keeping them? How long do they need?"

"Patience. We've waited this long, a half hour more isn't going to make any difference." Lane stood up, walked over to the window, and looked out at the massive asteroid that they had tamed. He considered the problems with the Outer Space Treaty, of which there were many. Under its current guise, there was nothing to stop another company just attaching itself to the far side of the AsterX asteroid and mining it. Not that anybody would, they were an exclusive club and had all, more or less, agreed on a set of unwritten rules. Nevertheless, everyone conceded that the treaty was grossly out of date. Formulated back in the late 60s, before Armstrong even put a boot print on the moon, it served, at least, to establish some international rules for the exploration of space and, more importantly, for the exploitation of its resources. But back when it was signed, the concept of a private company making it into space was laughable. But, to their credit, they had to consider that the possibility could exist sometime in the future, even if it was fanciful.

In short, no country could lay claim to any object in space. So when the US flag was hammered into the surface of the Moon, it wasn't to proclaim it as the fifty-first state. However, under the terms, you could dig a hole in it, and whatever you dug up you could keep. This was the basis that AsterX, and a bunch of other companies like them, operated under. The problem for private companies, though, was they needed oversight from a national government before they could do anything in space. So politics entered the arena. In Lane's mind it was almost medieval. To venture forth and explore needed the equivalent of a royal seal.

Of course private corporations were lobbying hard to remove the need for national oversight, but after all the shenanigans up on Mars, and the subsequent high-profile court case by COM, there were those who argued that national oversight was needed now more than ever. Others countered that what was really needed was a truly independent body to be set up to oversee and arbitrate all space exploration. With the rush to Mars now in full swing, the need to get clarity was even more urgent. To this end, a revision to the original 1967 Outer Space Treaty was to be discussed, and hopefully ratified, at a special UN session due to take place in a few months time.

But this was of no use to Lane Zebos and AsterX. They had to do it the old fashioned way, and that meant greasing the palms of a select number of gray and anonymous administrators in the key positions in government. A slow and frustratingly tedious process whose ultimate climax was, this very moment, being played out behind closed doors in the State Department.

So all Lane could do was wait until the session ended and the fate of the AsterX Mars mission would be revealed, but he wasn't expecting any surprises. The right moves had been made, so it should be a simple rubber stamping. Yet, you never truly knew for sure. Something might yet upset the fall of the dominoes that AsterX had so carefully set up.

So, for now the cigar was staying firmly in his top pocket.

LANE GLANCED over to the far side of the room to see Dr. Jane Foster, the chief medical officer, step onto the floor from the ceiling tunnel connecting this section of the torus with the central body of the mining station. It was a tricky transition from zero gravity at the center to one third G at the outer edge of the torus. The connecting tube was one of four spokes, with a ladder running inside its length. The trick was to enter it feet first at the start so you were oriented correctly when the centrifugal force began to kick in. Some people would make the mistake of entering head first, like climbing a ladder, only to realize they were effectively upside down when it was time to exit. It was a mistake you only made once.

Lane nodded to her as a greeting. She nodded back, then moved over and began to fix herself a coffee from the small galley. Finally she sat down beside them in one of the luxurious leather seats, tucked her feet up under her and sipped her drink. "Any word?"

They both looked at her in silence.

"I'll take that as a no, then."

Lane simply nodded.

"Oh, a bit of news for you. Xaing Zu Industries just landed on Mars."

"When?" said Chuck.

"About six hours ago. The news just came in, direct from Colony One. It's on their feed."

"How is that going down with them?" said Lane.

"Hard to say, it was just a one line announcement."

Chuck jotted down a quick calculation on the tablet he was holding. "If that's the case then COM will be... let's see... fourteen days behind, give or take."

"Should that not be sols?" Lane gave him a sideways grin.

"Sols, days, who cares. It just means we're going to be very late to the party."

"Well, that might be a good thing. Plenty of time for the other guests to get acquainted."

Chuck laughed. "Ha, that's one way of putting it. I

would say, at this rate there may be nothing for us to visit, even if we do get the go ahead."

Lane said nothing, just extracted the cigar canister from his top pocket again and repeated the same examination procedure as before.

"You're not thinking of lighting that up in here?" said Dr. Foster.

Lane just gave her a sideways smile.

"As the medical doctor assigned to this mission I would be negligent in my duties if I didn't inform you that inhaling tobacco smoke is a serious health risk." She sipped her coffee.

"I would say that going to Mars is a serious health risk." Lane held up the cigar. "This, on the other hand, is an art form."

Before the merits of cigar smoking could be discussed any further, an alert flashed on the main lounge monitor. They all stopped talking and focused on the screen. A head and shoulders materialized. It was Jake Lester, from the legal team, sitting at his desk back on Earth.

"Good news, the mission to salvage the ISA Odyssey Mars transit craft is a go."

The executive lounge on the AsterX mining station erupted into cheers, and high-fives, and hugs.

"Do we get to land?" Lane broke away from the celebrations and directed his question to Jake. There was a slight time delay as the message wound its way back to Earth.

"Yes."

More cheers and air punches ensued.

"There's just one caveat."

They stopped, and looked at the screen.

"You must do everything you can to bring home the ISA crewmember, Dr. Jann Malbec."

7

SEARCH

After a brief period of stilted pleasantries, the Xaing Zu expedition was assigned to an accommodation pod and left to themselves. Nevertheless, the pod was monitored by hidden cameras that fed back to the workstations in the central dais of the biodome. Gizmo had been charged with the task of monitoring their activity. So far, it all looked to be innocuous, at least on the surface. During the sols that followed, the Chinese settled in to a routine of survey and analysis of the colony's biology and infrastructure.

They had initially left two of their crew still onboard the landing craft, and from Jann's discussions with their commander, Jing Tzu, she ascertained that this was to ensure the craft was manned and ready to take off at any time. Of the six that now resided in the colony Jann had reckoned that two were geneticists/biologists and the rest seemed to be more military. This latter group spent their time surveying the facility, checking layouts, airlocks, power, operations, life support and a host of other inventory tasks. The biologists had taken up residence in the medlab where Jann had given them some space to work in. She had also gone into great detail with them about the various genetically engineered biomes that populated the colony and made it function. But it was clear to all that what they were truly looking for was the genetic understanding of what gave Jann and all the other colonists their remarkable healing abilities and youthful demeanor.

The Chinese, to their credit, had tried to work within the restrictions placed on them by the colonists, but with each passing sol they pushed at the boundaries. There had been a lot of friction and even a punch up or two, but for the most part they tried to do what they came here to do without killing anyone, at least so far. Nonetheless, time was running out for them. No doubt there were powerful people behind this enterprise applying pressure on Jing Tzu to come up with the goods. And the situation was going to get increasingly more difficult for all concerned once COM set foot in the colony. Because as soon as that happened, they would legally own it, and everything belonging to it. Jing Tzu and Xaing Zu Industries would be booted out and their mission would fail. All this Jann knew, but she also knew that a cornered rat was a dangerous animal, ready to strike out. And Jing Tzu was being backed into an impossible corner.

.   .   .

JANN WAS CURRENTLY in the medlab, checking on a new data set she had recently received, when Jing Tzu entered. He looked over at one of the Chinese techs and said something in Mandarin that Jann could not understand.

"You're wasting your time, you know." Jann directed her comment at the commander. He looked at her with an air of disdain.

"I keep telling you," Jann continued, "the knowledge you're looking for no longer exists."

"So you keep saying." Jing Tzu finally managed.

"Yet you keep looking. And now time is running out, isn't it?" Jann was baiting him.

Jing Tzu stood for a moment and considered her, then sat down on the other side of the bench where Jann was working.

"You could help us. You could let us conduct some tests on the colonists here."

"That's not going to happen. You know that. If you were to start that, then all hell would break loose. Remember these colonists have already been through one tough fight to get their freedom so they don't take kindly to being pushed around. As it is there are those who are itching to kick you all out onto the planet's surface and leave you there."

Jing Tzu sighed. "They must understand that we are here to help you. We are not the enemy."

Jann laughed. "Bullshit. You're here for one thing and one thing only. We all know that."

"Then help us."

"By letting you experiment on the colony population?"

"Just tests, to get an understanding of the underlying physiological changes that have occurred here."

"You just don't get it, do you? This will not help you find what you are looking for. The Janus bacterium that causes this... physical transformation was eradicated a long time ago." Jann waved her hand in the air. "Which is lucky for you because if it wasn't then some of your crew would be raging psychopaths, out to kill everyone in their path."

Jing Tzu abruptly stood up and pointed a finger at Jann. "You are a fool if you think this is all there is to it. COM are landing in less than a week, don't think they will be as accommodating as we are. You are going to need some friends when they get here, because *they* are going to find it with or without your help. So I suggest you go and think about that for a while." He walked out of the medlab leaving Jann to contemplate the shit storm that was coming down the track.

THIS ENCOUNTER with Jing Tzu had left Jann feeling distracted, but she tried to put it out of her mind and focus on her work. For a long time she had been cataloging the many GM bacteria that were utilized within the colony environment, everything from soil processing to fuel manufacture. A good deal of this work had been done already, with the help of scientists back on Earth. Jann had built up an extensive network of academics interested in the development of the Mars colony. She had just received a theoretical analysis on how a particular bacterium could be modified to improve CO_2 breakdown. She tried to reread the paper but could not keep her concentration for long.

It didn't help that Nills had had to return to Colony Two. Some technical emergency with one of the thermal heat exchangers that only he could fix. Perhaps that's what made her so tetchy, made her bait Jing Tzu like that. Nills had left that morning, on the bed, flying off across the crater in a cloud of dust, leaving Jann to contend with the ever invasive investigations of the Chinese crew. He vowed to return before COM landed, as that would be a pivotal moment. In accordance with the ruling from the International Court of Arbitration, once they set foot in the colony it would automatically return to their ownership. Since the Chinese were currently operating under the public domain legality that had been established by the ISA, they were going to get booted out by COM—first item on the agenda. How would they react to this, considering the pressure they were under to source the Janus bacteria? This was a question that greatly troubled the entire colony. Would they go quietly? Would they try and negotiate with COM? Or would a fight begin? And where would the colonists fall in all of this? What would happen to them?

. . .

HER THOUGHTS WERE INTERRUPTED by Gizmo whizzing into the medlab.

"Jann, could you possibly spare me a moment of your time?" Jann looked at the quirky robot. She understood what it was really saying to her. *I have something important to reveal, in private, away from prying eyes.*

"Sure. Let's take a walk." She rose from her workbench and they headed out of the medlab towards the biodome. They zigzagged their way though the rows of hydroponics and finally entered one of the food processing rooms. These were small landers attached to the main biodome used for sorting and packing of harvested produce. They had chosen this place because of its isolation and also because the processing machines made quite a racket when switched on. Jann closed the door behind them and looked over at Gizmo.

A light flickered on from Gizmo's breastplate and a video image was projected on the wall. It was an aerial view of the surface of Mars.

"When Nills was making his trip to Colony Two this morning he detoured over the Chinese lander. This is what he saw."

Jann watched as the craft came into view. The video was taken from quite high up, Nills had obviously decided to be as unobtrusive as possible. Then it zoomed in on the base of the craft. On the surface two small mobile units could be seen parked close to the foot of the craft. Mounted on these were what looked to Jann to be artillery weapons.

"Nills reckons that these are PEP's. Pulsed Energy Projectile weapons, with considerable range. He asked me to contact him as soon as you have seen this video. I will try and make the connection now."

A new picture-in-picture image was projected on the wall. It was Nills facing the camera.

"Jann, you saw that, did you?"

"Yeah, what do you make of it?"

"It looks like you were right. They're carrying a lot of very sophisticated weaponry."

"Jesus, they're armed to the teeth."

"Yeah, so I'd say they're here for the long haul. They're not leaving without a fight."

Jann looked at the grainy image for a moment, digesting the implications of this discovery. Xaing Zu Industries had come prepared to battle it out if necessary. And it was safe to assume they had even more weapons, probably handheld.

"Nills, you'd better get back here as soon as you can."

"Yeah, once I can get this heat exchanger sorted out."

"Okay, but don't leave it too long. We need to formulate a plan on how best to deal with the possibility of a firefight between COM and the Chinese."

"I know." Nills signed off and Gizmo stopped the projection.

"Have you had any luck hacking into their comms, Gizmo?"

"None. Other than I established that their systems are encrypted using quantum entanglement."

"What does that mean?"

"It is impossible to crack."

Jann considered this for a moment. "We have grossly underestimated them, Gizmo."

"It would seem so."

"It now looks like a war is about to start."

8

FIRE

Lieutenant Dan Ma of the Xaing Zu Mars mission scanned the row of EVA suits that hung from makeshift hangers along one wall of the accommodation pod that the colonists had assigned them. Having located his suit, he reached into the side section and released the clip on the concealed compartment. He withdrew a small electronic unit and flicked the switch. All cameras and audio devices within this general area would now be jammed. It was a precaution, but one worth taking. Next he withdrew a bulkier unit, examined it, and placed it carefully inside the pocket of his flight suit. With COM due to land very soon, and their own mission no further along in accomplishing their primary objective, it was time to take assertive action.

It was mid-afternoon and the colonists were busy

with their various tasks. Mostly they would be in the biodome tending to food production. It seemed to be their primary job, that and the maintenance of life support. In many ways, he admired them. Particularly considering what they had already been through. To survive up here, on this godforsaken rock, took a special kind of person. One who understood the fragility of life, who tended to its needs with diligence and dedication. Nothing was ever taken for granted. You survived by the sweat of your brow. It was life on the edge, one false move and it could be extinguished in a heartbeat. But time was running out, and there was no more room for sentimentality.

Some of the colonists eyed him with suspicion as he passed. They did not like them being here. He couldn't blame them, if they only knew what was in store they would have never let them inside in the first place. He ignored their looks and continued deeper into the biodome. Over the last few sols he and his team had planned for this moment to have the maximum effect. They had pored over the facilities schematics, probing, testing, finding the perfect spot to install the device where it would give them the best chance of success. They had ascertained that the optimum location was at the very far end of the biodome, beside a number of the food-processing pods, where a lot of storage crates had been stacked.

He had to circle around a few times so as to ensure the area was empty of colonists when he arrived. On the third approach he got his chance. He ducked in behind the crates and withdrew the device from his pocket. He set the timer and then carefully placed it near the center of the stack. Job done, time to leave. He absolutely did not want to be here when this thing went off.

NILLS HAD BEEN AWAY for several sols, and still not returned. So, with the imminent arrival of COM, Jann was getting anxious. She sat at the workstation in the medlab trying to concentrate on her work, something to take her mind off the uncertainty that lay ahead. She was alone in the lab, save for Gizmo, who was preparing DNA samples for her. A tediously repetitive task that the robot was ideally suited for. The Chinese had brought a DNA sequencer with them and Jann had decided to put it to good use. She had struggled with much of her analysis through lack of this type of equipment. Now that it was here she would make good use of it. The Chinese lab techs were not around, the place was hers. Xenon had observed them leaving Colony One early that morning, ostensibly to retrieve more supplies from their craft. They would need to be checked and searched on return, before anything was allowed into the facility. Xenon had been designated to this responsibility, one in which he was admirably suited due to his imposing physique. He would ensure that no weapons were brought on site.

But, there was still no definitive answer from COM as

to their expected landing time. They were already in orbit, and had been for some time now. But they were being very circumspect in their communication. The colonists had planned to meet them on the surface, a welcoming party of sorts, like they did with the Xaing Zu mission. But, COM were not interested in this, in fact they seemed openly hostile to it. This irked Jann no end. Who did they think they were? They had an arrogance that implied that the colonists were not important in the Colony One Mars consortium's worldview. Jann reckoned that this was probably true. It angered her, and the more she thought about it the angrier she got. Who the hell did they think they were? How were they even allowed to set foot on this planet after all they had done? The destruction of the original ISA mission was due, in no small part, to the treachery of COM and its agent Annis Romanov. Not to mention the horror of the cloning tanks in Colony Two being a result of their vision for genetic research. Although, one could argue, that COM was not in direct control of the insane Dr. Vanji. Nevertheless, once they were aware of what was going on up here, they openly embraced it.

But what angered Jann the most was the fact that the courts on Earth saw fit to hand it all back to them. It was a morally repugnant concept to Jann, which reinforced in her the feeling that Earth had abandoned them, once again.

"Jann... Jann."

"Uh... Gizmo, sorry, I was just... somewhere else."

"Your hand, it is bleeding."

"What?" Jann looked down. She had been so distracted by her thoughts that she had accidentally cut herself with the scalpel. She opened her fingers and let the blood drop on to the workbench. She wrapped a bandage around the hand to staunch the bleeding. "Any word from Nills?"

"None. Would you like me to open a communications channel with Colony Two?"

"No. It's okay. Leave him be. He'll contact us when he's ready. Although he's cutting it fine. COM are due to land soon."

"Very well."

Jann was just finished tending to her hand when an ear-splitting klaxon blasted out from all corners of the colony facility.

"What the hell is that?"

"Fire alarm. Emanating in the biodome, far end, near the food processing pods."

"Shit, fire... come on, let's go."

They raced out of the medlab heading for the biodome. Fire in an enclosed environment such as Colony One could be disastrous if not extinguished quickly. If left to grow, it would suck in all the oxygen, and had the potential to seriously compromise life support. Every colonist and astronaut's worst fear was fire. You died, not from burning, but suffocation.

Others were also racing towards the source of the fire, having been trained to drop everything and focus on putting out any fire that started as quickly as humanly possible. By the time Jann and Gizmo had reached the food processing pods, it looked like the entire population of the colony was already there. The storage crates stacked along the inner wall of the biodome were completely ablaze. Flame blossomed out from the center of the stack and the air was filled with the oddly sweet smell of burning bio-plastic. Jann could see Xenon marshaling a group of colonists with water hoses. He shouted and waved as they wrestled with the apparatus. Finally a jet of frothy H_2O burst out and the colonists began to douse the flames. It didn't take long to get it under control, and within a few minutes the drama was over. As the colonists began to gather up the firefighting equipment Jann and Xenon tentatively approached the smoldering pile.

"How the hell did that happen?"

"I don't know." Xenon picked up a lump of melted plastic. "This stuff takes a lot to burn. You would need a sustained flame to get it going like that."

Jann toed something on the ground, hidden in a mound of debris. She reached down, and with the help of a pen she had pulled from her pocket, she prodded the unit free from the pile, all the time covering her mouth and nose to try and lessen the effects of the smoke, and the sickly sweet smell of burnt bio-plastic. She poked the pen through a loop of charred wire that protruded from the unit and held it up. Xenon looked over at her. "What have you got there?"

Jann shuffled through the group of colonists that were busy cleaning up the mess, holding the unit out in front of her like she had discovered a dead rat and was disposing of it. She laid it down at the edge of the path just as Xenon came over. They both knelt down and Jann started knocking the dust and ash from the unit.

"I could be mistaken, Xenon, but this does *not* look like food to me." She picked it up and examined it. It was small, about the size of a pack of cigarettes, on one side a charred circuit board was attached to a rectangular container which was split and broken.

"You think this is an incendiary device, you think somebody started this fire deliberately?" Xenon was now inspecting the device.

"Sure looks that way. But why would anyone want to do that?"

Xenon just looked at her blankly.

"We need to contact Nills, maybe he can shed some light on who might have built this." She handed the device to Gizmo who took it gently in its metal hand. "Can you get some images off to Nills and explain to him what happened."

"Will do," said Gizmo.

By now some of the other colonists had spotted them and came over. "Is someone trying to burn the place down? Have we got some crazy pyromaniac on our hands now? Jesus, that's all we need."

Xenon looked around. "It's okay, let's just get this place sorted."

He started getting the colonists busy again, issuing directions and organizing them into cleanup groups.

"Jann, may I have a word with you?" said Gizmo.

She looked at the quirky droid. Generally when Gizmo said may I have a word with you, it was never good.

"Sure, Gizmo. Let's go over here a bit and we can talk."

They moved off away from the throng of colonists who were now busy sweeping, picking and sorting through the mess that was left after the fire. "What is it, Gizmo?"

"I cannot seem to raise a communication channel with Colony Two."

"Has the fire damaged comms?"

"No. That would be highly improbable."

"Then what?"

"I am being prevented from accessing it."

"Prevented?"

"Yes, blocked. I cannot access a comms channel and what's more, I cannot access any of the Colony One systems."

"Are you serious?"

"I assure you Jann, this is not one of my attempts at humor."

Before Jann could interrogate Gizmo any further, a colonist came rushing into the crowd. "Can someone give me a hand? The entrance door is jammed and I can't get open, I need some help."

Ever since Jann had been in Colony One, and that was several years, she had never seen the tunnel door to the biodome closed, save for one time when she herself had forced it closed, to prevent the demented Decker from beating her head in. So, if the door was closed then someone had to have closed it—deliberately.

"We'll give you a hand. Gizmo come with us." They dashed through the biodome to the far side and Jann could see the door shut tight. She threw her weight behind the locking wheel but it was stuck even with Gizmo and the other colonist helping her, there was no moving the wheel. *What the hell is going on?* she thought.

By now others had gathered around, and a sense of entrapment was beginning to build. They took turns to try and open it, but it refused to budge no matter how much muscle power was brought to bear on the locking mechanism.

Xenon arrived with a party of colonists. "What's going on"?

"The door's jammed, we're locked in, there's no other way out of here," said one of the colonists.

"I think Xaing Zu have locked us in here deliberately," said another.

"What? Why would they do that?" The colonists were confused.

"Gizmo can't raise a comm channel or get access to any Colony One systems. The droid has been blocked."

"Oh shit, they're going to kill us all, gas us while we're all trapped in here." A sense of panic was beginning to build, as a number of them started to bang on the steel door.

"This is your fault." A colonist pointed an accusatory finger at Jann. "It was you who convinced us to allow them in. We should have never listened to you. Now we're all going to die."

Xenon moved in front of Jann and raised a hand. "This is not the time to lose your cool. That isn't helping anyone."

The colonists were panicking, banging the door, shouting. Things were becoming ugly.

"Attention." A disembodied voice echoed out from the overhead speakers and reverberated around the biodome. *"Please be calm. We have secured you in the biodome for your own protection. Do not be alarmed. You are safe in here while we negotiate this transition."*

"Screw you," a colonist shook her fist at the speaker. "Let us out of here, you bastards."

Xenon signaled to Jann and they took a short walk, out of earshot of the other colonists. "COM must have landed and Xaing Zu knew about it. My guess is the fire was a way to get us all in here. They knew our emergency fire protocols, knew we would all drop everything and run in to the biodome."

"But why?" Said Jann.

"To get us all out of the way while they prepare to defend the facility."

"They're not going to let COM have access, are they?"

"Unlikely."

"This is not good, Xenon."

"No. I fear we are trapped. They have tricked us, and now we are powerless to intervene."

9

COM

Of the three heat exchangers that provided power for Colony Two, only one now functioned, and that had broken down twice in the last month. Nills used the other units that were offline to scavenge parts, just so he could keep this one going. Systems were breaking down all the time. Already they had shut down significant areas within Colony Two, they simply did not have the resources to keep everything maintained. Worse, this technological disintegration was also being mirrored in the slow physical and mental degradation of the colonists.

Nills had hoped that the arrival of Xaing Zu and COM would bring with them sufficient supplies and spare parts to enable, at least, a partial rejuvenation of the colony. But what the Chinese brought with them was merely a drop in the bucket. Nills felt that they were just paying lip service to the requirements of the colonists, as if in reality, they were not that important. Perhaps he had been naive, as Jann had often said to him. *You're too nice. Nills. You believe that humans are genuinely good. But in my experience, everybody wants something, and it's generally not your well being.* He found it hard to be that cynical, even if there was a grain of truth in it. Yet, soon COM would land, if they hadn't already. It was hard to know as the communication was as sparse as it was terse. They had offered to bring supplies and badly needed spare parts. Hopefully they would be true to their word and Nills could get his hands on these, before everything went to rat-shit.

Nills checked the seals on the replacement pump one last time, and then nodded to Anika, who was monitoring the starters for the heat exchanger on the control panel.

"Can you try it again now?"

With that, Anika set the controls to activate the newly replaced pump and reroute pressure back into the turbine.

"Okay, here goes." She hit the switch, and slowly the turbine started spinning up. She gave Nills the thumbs up. He gathered up his tools and joined her over at the control board, checking stats on the readouts.

"Okay, it's back up again, but for how long, who knows. Anyway, let's close up shop here, and head back up to operations. We'll see if there's been any news on COM."

With the colony being low on power for the last while, the temperature inside had dropped noticeably. It didn't help that a sandstorm had been building outside, reducing the efficiency of the solar array field. If Nills and Anika hadn't managed to fix the heat exchanger they would be in real trouble. It seemed to Nills that the threat of these life-and-death scenarios were being overlooked in the climate of uncertainty that had enveloped the colony ever since the arrival of Xaing Zu. When Nills finally arrived in the operations room, he had wrapped himself up in a long brown coat that he had become very attached to. It was old and worn and how it came to be here, in the colony, or even how it came into his possession he had long forgotten. Holburn looked up from his console when he spotted Nills entering. "Good work on that heat exchanger, not a moment too soon either. Storm is getting pretty bad out there. Any longer and we'd be running on fumes."

"Any word on COM?"

"Yes and no. They dropped out of orbit about two hours ago, but I've had no comms and no confirmation of touchdown."

"You think the sandstorm is affecting comms?"

"Possibly. It can do that, if it gets bad enough."

Nills sat down at the table and shoved his hands into his coat pockets to get some warmth back into them. "Did you try to contact Colony One and see if they've heard anything?"

"I can't get through to them either."

"This is not really going to plan, is it?"

Holburn looked over at Nills and shrugged. "Could be worse, maybe COM crash landed and everyone is dead."

Nills gave him back a sideways grin. "Problem solved, then."

"Oh, nearly forgot." Holburn passed a holo-tab over to Nills. "One message did come through, about an hour ago, from your friend, Lane Zebos, AsterX."

Nills picked up the tab and tapped an icon. It was a video message. Nills tapped again to bring it up on the main screen. It was a head and shoulders shot of the AsterX CEO inside their cramped spacecraft. Of all the expeditions en route to Mars these guys were definitely the poor cousins. But, they were also the least threatening, concerning themselves more with the mineralogy and the technical capabilities of Mars, and Colony Two in particular. Understandable, considering that they were a mining company. Where Jann, Xenon and the rest of the council had concerned themselves with countering the machinations of Xaing Zu and COM, Nills had found Lane Zebos to be more like himself. Interested in the technicalities of the colony: its functioning, its resources. They were also the only one of the three that took a deep interest in bringing what Nills had wanted in terms of equipment, supplies and spare parts. But since they were not seen as a direct threat, the council had spent very little time communicating with them, leaving it to Nills to deal with their queries. As a result Nills had built up a reasonably friendly relationship with Zebos, who was now on screen.

The good news is we have embarked with all of the items you have requested. Some are bit hard to come by, but where we couldn't source the exact item we have endeavored to acquire a substitute. I've also added in a little gift for you. You'll see it on the manifest attached. Nills started reading down through the list.

That's the good news. The bad news is we won't be in Mars orbit for another eight weeks, give or take. It took us a long time to secure the necessary oversight. But we're on our way now, so see you all in two months. That's it for now. Will keep you posted. The message ended.

Anika had entered the operations room as the Zebos message was on screen, and had taken a seat beside Nills. "So what's the *little gift,* then?"

Nills pushed the tab over to her and pointed to the last two lines on the manifest.

"Ten kilos of Blue Mountain coffee and a case of twenty-five year old Scotch." Anika read it aloud.

Nills smiled. "I, for one, cannot wait. I count the days until they land."

"What, nothing for the girls? You know, silk stockings, a few ounces of Coco Chanel, perhaps."

Nills took the tab back, looked at the list again, and spun it back to Anika, and pointed at an entry higher up in the manifest. It read, *5lbs Belgian Chocolates.* "Your favorite, if I'm not mistaken."

"Oooh..." said Anika.

"Hey guys, you'd better take a look at this." Holburn's fingers danced across the face of his control pad and a new image materialized on screen. A ghostly cloud of dust filled the monitor and from its center an image of a rover emerged, moving slowly towards them. The trio watched in silence for a few moments.

"That's outside the main airlock here in Colony Two."

"Yep, but that's not one of our rovers, too big."

"COM?" Said Nills.

They looked from one to the other. Then comms burst into life.

Colony Two, this is Commander Willem Kruger, of the Colony One Mars consortium, seeking permission to enter.

"Holy crap," said Anika. "What do we do?"

Nills stood up. "Goddammit, this was not part of the plan. This was not supposed to happen."

"What are they doing? Why didn't they contact us and let us know they were landing?" said Holburn.

"Because we would be better prepared. They want us off balance."

"So what do we do? Tell them the store is closed, come back tomorrow?" said Anika.

"No, it makes no difference whether it's now, tomorrow, next week. We have to face this sometime, may as well be now." Nills was on his feet now. "Holburn, tell them we're opening the airlock. Anika, you come with me. We'll gather up the reception party and meet them in the main entrance. Make sure everyone is armed."

Nills realized they had been thrown a curveball. What everyone thought COM would do, they had just gone and done the opposite. He should have known not to trust them. They were trying to gain the upper hand and they knew that leaving them outside on the surface was not an option. At least not a very good one.

"Are you expecting trouble?" said Anika.

"You need to understand that as far as the people in that rover are concerned, they own this place, and everything in it. That includes us—you, me and everyone in here. So yeah, I'm expecting trouble if we don't do what they want."

BY THE TIME they got to the entrance cavern other colonists were beginning to gather. The COM rover had been left waiting outside the entrance airlock, as the colonists got themselves organized. Anika was now distributing weapons from one of the storage rooms at the back entrance cavern. These were mainly railguns, kept primed and ready for action.

"I want two up there, high on the gantry, one on each side. And two more at the back of the cavern, high up on those storage crates over there. Keep your weapons visible, let them see we're armed."

As the colonists left to take up their positions, others gathered round Nills and Anika who had taken up a central position facing the airlock entrance.

"Okay, let's do this." Nills tapped his earpiece to talk to Holburn, who was monitoring the situation from the operations room. "You can open the airlock now."

From inside the cavern they could hear the rumble of

the exterior door opening to expose the inner airlock to the maelstrom outside. A few moments later they heard the rumble again to signify that the COM rover had now entered. A few tense moments passed as the volume within was repressurized and the dust and sand purged through the scrubbers.

Nills tapped his earpiece again. "Tell them to exit the rover inside the airlock before we open the door."

Nills looked up and around at the people he had positioned on high ground within the cavern.

"Okay, everyone ready?"

A chorus of *ready* echoed around the space. Nills turned back to face the door and tapped his earpiece again. "Okay Holburn, ready when you are."

Anxious moments passed as they waited, and waited. Finally they heard motors kick in as the inner airlock door started to rise to reveal six COM crew members in full EVA suits—all armed to the teeth.

"Holy crap," said Anika.

Nills raised his hand and stepped forward. Then one of the COM crew popped open his visor, and stepped forward.

"Welcome to Mars," said Nills. Then he pointed at them. "Now I would ask you to put down your weapons as they are not allowed inside the colony."

"I am commander Willem Kruger, and you are?"

"Nills Langthorp."

Kruger looked around the entrance cavern, spotting

the elevated positions of the weapons that were trained on them.

"Ahh... The famous Nills Langthorp, in the flesh. Do you realize that you're a legend back on Earth?"

Nills took another step forward. "I would appreciate if you would put away those weapons."

Kruger smiled. "Let's not start off on the wrong foot. We were expecting a better welcome than this." He looked around at the assembled colonists, who were becoming decidedly twitchy.

"I think perhaps a little demonstration might be in order." With that he lifted a small handheld weapon and fired at one of the colonists high up in the gantry. A burst of incandescent brilliance strobed the cavern as the colonist was encased in a mesh of flashing light. He shook violently and then fell from his position down onto a plastic crate with a thump. This resulted in the colonists directing a hail of fire at the six COM crewmembers, who were also returning fire. All around Nills and Anika colonists were engulfed in flashing balls of plasma. The cavern reverberated with the sounds of shrieking and whoomp, whoomp from the weapons of the COM crew.

Nills shouted, "Stop, stop, cease fire."

The six COM crew stood exactly where they were, as if nothing had happened, the colonists' railguns having had absolutely no effect against the armour of their EVA suits. They stood and faced off against each other as the realization slowly sank in to the colonists that they were completely defenseless.

"Like I said, let's not start off on the wrong foot. There is nothing you have that can threaten us. So why don't you all just drop your weapons and behave. You'll find your fallen comrades to be just temporarily paralyzed, they'll come to—eventually."

Nills knew there was no point in fighting. They were totally outclassed. So he turned around to the colonists still standing. "Put down the weapons. Nothing will be gained by any more fighting." And he threw his own weapon on the ground in front of the commander. One by one the colonists followed suit. The battle was over. They had lost.

The COM mercenaries began to split them up into groups and then started herding them back in to the main cavern in Colony Two, carrying their fallen comrades as they went. It was clear to Nills that COM had detailed knowledge of its layout. They knew where to go, how to get there and what to do to keep complete control of the situation. He was about to fall into line with the others when the commander came over and tapped his shoulder. Nills spun around.

"Mr. Langthorp. If you would be so kind as to follow me."

"Where to?"

"This way, into the rover. We're going on a little journey. There is someone who very much wants to meet you."

10

VANHOFF

Nills sat in the back of the rover as it bounced over the surface. Outside, the Martian world was obscured by a thick cloud of dust. The driver navigated through this impenetrable fog by virtue of a heads-up display overlaid across the entire front windscreen. The oncoming topography rendered itself in grainy detail like seeing the world through a old fashioned video game. To Nills, the machine had a distinct military design about it: sparse, utilitarian, and crammed with technical wizardry. Facing him, on the opposite side of the rover, Commander Kruger sat clutching a short but bulky weapon across his lap.

"Pulsed Energy Projectile, if I'm not mistaken." Nills nodded at the weapon. Kruger gave a sideways grin and gripped the weapon closer.

"Very good, right on the money. How did you know that?"

"I read about them. Interesting technology. Although, the ones I looked at needed a truck to carry them around."

Kruger held up the weapon and examined it like it was a treasured possession. "Things have moved on a bit since then."

THE PROBLEM with ballistic weapons in any space environment is similar to that in an aircraft with a pressurized cabin. There is a strong likelihood of puncturing the delicate fabric of the hull and suffering a catastrophic loss of internal pressure. The problem of course, is far greater in space because, at least with the aircraft you could technically still be alive while you plummeted to your death from 10,000 ft. In space however, you died almost instantly just from the decompression, not to mention lack of oxygen and sub-zero temperatures.

So when it became apparent to the powers that be that a different type of weapon would be required by any future spacefaring law enforcement agency, the task fell to DARPA to come up with a solution. Some argued that there should be no need for this sort of thing at all. Others said just keep it simple, and go back to using bows and arrows. But this didn't fit very well with the high-tech space exploration image.

As luck would have it, DARPA happened to have something that might fit the bill, something they had been working on for quite some time. It came about from the desire of terrestrial agencies for a non-lethal weapon. Something they could use in riots and general public disorder situations where killing the actual protagonists would be... well, overkill.

It was called a Pulsed Energy Projectile Weapon, or simple PEP. It utilized a high-energy laser pulse that created a small plasma explosion on impact. This explosion created an electromagnetic shock wave that stunned the target. Because it relied on electrical energy rather than a projectile to get the job done, it could be used with relative safety in the enclosed confines of a space station, with little risk of puncturing a hole in the outer skin. Although, it would do a good job of frying any electronics that happened to be in the way.

So far so good. The only downside was it weighed in at a hefty 250kg, about the weight of three men, and needed a truck to carry it around. Nevertheless, their early developments were dusted off and over time it became lighter and deadlier. The variants that the COM mercenaries used were still a good deal heavier than even a fully tooled up Browning M2, but in one-third G, that really didn't matter. They also could be lethal, although they did come with a very handy knob allowing you to adjust the level of deadliness, dialing it down from *lethal* to *paralyze* to *stun*.

It was a revolutionary weapon, particularly for crowd control. No longer did security personnel need to be hesitant, they could take out large numbers of aggressors with impunity. It made it viable for a small number of well armed individuals to safely deal with a much larger number of subjects. In Commander Kruger's mind, it was the weapon that made this mission possible.

"SO WHERE ARE WE GOING?" Nills already knew the answer to this. Let's face it, there were not many places on Mars you could go. But he had Kruger talking, so decided to keep probing.

"Back to the ship. Somebody wants to meet you."

"Somebody too important to risk entering the colony facility."

"Yeah, something like that." It was a hesitant reply.

"So you haven't entered Colony One then?"

Kruger stayed silent for a minute, sizing Nills up. "I'm sure he'll fill you in when you meet."

The driver cocked his head around. "Commander, ETA in one minute."

Nills looked at the heads up display. A new shape was beginning to format itself in the gloom, it was big. And since it was still one minute away, it must be very big indeed.

By the time they arrived Nills realized that big was too small a word for it. The only thing he saw outside through the windshield was a gigantic landing strut as they passed on the right hand side of it. Ahead of them a gantry had been lowered, presumably from the underside of the ship. Yellow lights flashed and illuminated the clouds of dust that had been whipped up in the storm. The rover drove straight onto the gantry platform, came to a halt, and then started to slowly ascend—into the belly of the whale.

A few moments later, Nills stepped out of the rover and into a compact utilitarian loading bay. It was crammed full of equipment and machines, they were anticipating a long stay. As he looked around the ship he considered just how far things had progressed since the early days of the first colonist landings. They had all been packed like sardines into tiny craft. *How long ago was that now,* he wondered. *Over a decade?*

"This way." Kruger ushered him across the loading bay to a ladder leading up into the interior of the craft.

"Follow me." He started climbing up. Nills followed. They passed up through a number of levels until finally they stepped off into an operations area. Several crewmembers occupied various workstations around the perimeter of the space. They all stopped what they were doing and turned around to look at Nills. In the middle of the room, sitting at a circular holo-table was a gaunt looking old man.

"Nills Langthorp, a pleasure to meet you. Please have a seat." The old man signaled to an empty chair on the opposite side of the holo-table. Nills obliged.

He leaned in and studied Nills for a moment. "Incredible. To know of your existence is one thing, but to see you in the flesh is another thing entirely."

"Let me guess," said Nills. "Peter VanHoff, head honcho of the Colony One Mars consortium."

VanHoff gave a thin smile. "Very good, you are correct. How did you guess?"

"To know of your existence is one thing, but to see you in the flesh, well..."

VanHoff stopped smiling.

"So what do you want with me?" Nills continued.

VanHoff waved a dismissive hand. "Later. In the meantime I just want you where I can see you, out of harm's way."

"Why, is there going to be some harm?"

VanHoff shifted in his seat. "It seems our Oriental friends are being somewhat obstinate. Things could get a little... fractious, shall we say. They have battened down the hatches in Colony One and are refusing to cede authority."

"So they've given you the middle finger, then."

"Mere petulance on their part. I assure you we will regain control of what is rightfully ours."

"And what about the colonists?"

"That's what we would like to know. Whose side are they on?"

"They're on nobody's side. They just want to live in peace."

"Don't we all, Mr. Langthorp."

Nills stood up. "Well, it was nice talking to you, Peter. Let's do it again sometime. Now, if you don't mind I could do with a lift back."

VanHoff laughed. "Fascinating. You are a character, I'll give you that." His face stiffened. "Now sit down, you're not going anywhere."

Nills surveyed the room, several of the crew were gathered around, ready for action. Nills sighed, and sat down again. "Maybe I could stay a bit longer, then."

"Very good. Now, to answer your question. You are here for two reasons. Firstly, if the Chinese don't cooperate, and accept the ruling of the courts, then we will simply take over Colony One through force of arms. What I need you to do is settle the clones down, and make sure they don't do anything foolish."

"You mean the colonists."

"You know what I mean. Let's not make this any more difficult that it needs to be."

"What about Dr. Malbec? How are you planning to get her on your side?"

VanHoff's lips tightened. "Leave Malbec to me. She is the primary cause of all this mayhem—and she needs to pay for it."

Nills jumped up, leaned across the holo-table and gripped VanHoff by the lapels. "Over my dead body, you twisted little shit."

The crew scrambled to drag Nills off. He let go of VanHoff, just as a few thousand volts from a cattle prod shot through his body. He collapsed back down on the seat, his arm was twisted back and held tight by one of the crew. VanHoff dusted himself off and regained his composure. "I see you are a little upset. I appreciate that change can be disconcerting for all concerned. But you'll get used to it, eventually."

The pain that had engulfed Nills' body was subsiding and he too had regained some composure. "So what's the second one? You said there were two reasons I was here?"

VanHoff smiled. "Ah... yes. Indeed I did. You see, Nills. You are rather special. You are the reason we are all here fighting on this godforsaken rock. You are the key— and you always were."

"And what if I were to tell you to go shove it up your ass?"

VanHoff scowled and turned to Kruger. "Take him below and keep him secure."

THEY TOOK Nills and locked him in a small accommodation compartment on one of the lower levels of the craft. The room was compact, with a bed and not much else. He reckoned that it must have been regarded as first class digs on this ship, so he should feel privileged. The first half hour of his incarceration Nills spent examining every possible nook and cranny, looking for anything that he could find and use to his advantage. He didn't find anything. Eventually he sat down on the bed and considered what his next course of action should be. That was assuming that he even had a choice in the matter.

So VanHoff had made the trip himself, that much was evident. *But why would he do that?* Nills wondered. Maybe it was simply a case of, *if you want to do something right, then you just gotta do it yourself.* Every effort VanHoff had made so far to acquire the Janus bacteria had been thwarted by Dr. Jann Malbec. So she was number one on his hit list, he even said so himself. On top of that he expressed a clear disdain for the *clones* in Colony One. Whether they lived or died seemed to be of little interest to VanHoff. As for Xaing Zu? They really had no idea how outclassed they were by the resources that COM had brought to the planet. VanHoff just didn't care a damn for the lives in Colony One. Nills had to find a way to warn them. This was his number one task. Find a way to get a message to them—somehow.

GATHERED around the holo-table in the operations room of the COM craft sat VanHoff, Commander Willem Kruger and several others of the crew. Kruger cleared his throat and spoke. "Phase one of the operation is now complete. Colony Two is in our control and the clone specimen Langthorp has been acquired. Time now to move on to phase two. Are we ready?"

"Please proceed." VanHoff waved a hand.

"Raising a channel now, sir." One of the operatives tapped several icons on the holo-table. A 3D rendering of the COM logo materialized and rotated. *Channel open... waiting for connection... connection established.* The rotating logo was replaced with a video feed from inside the operations room in Colony One. Several Chinese sat around a similar holo-table.

Kruger cleared his throat again and spoke. "This is Commander Willem Kruger, of the Colony One Mars consortium mission. Please be advised that we have entered and secured the mining outpost, known as Colony Two, located at the northern edge of the Jezero Crater. In doing so we have now fulfilled the obligations required by the International Court of Arbitration for full ownership of the Colony One facilities to revert to COM ownership. Therefore, you are now trespassing on our property and we would be obliged if you would vacate the facility immediately. If you fail to do so within the next twelve hours then we will remove you by force. Do you understand this message?"

The figures around the corresponding holo-table in Colony One sat unmoved. There was a moment of tense silence before they replied. "*This is Commander Jing Tzu, of Xaing Zu Industries Mars mission. We understand your claim is issued by a terrestrial court which we do not recognize. Therefore we see your request as invalid and furthermore your threats to use force are taken as an act of aggression against a peaceful enterprise. We have claimed this facility under salvage and, as such, are legally entitled to remain. Any attempt by your people to gain access will be seen as trespassing on Xaing Zu property and will be repelled, with force if necessary. Do you understand this message?*"

Commander Kruger clasped his hands together and slowly leaned in across the holo-table. "You have twelve hours to leave." The video feed went dead and they all took a moment before VanHoff finally spoke.

"What's your assessment, Commander—are they bluffing?"

"We have to assume that they are not bluffing and have convinced themselves that they can hold it. Which means we need to reassess their capability and recalibrate our strategy to take control of Colony One."

"We need to keep damage to the facility to a minimum. Rebuilding it is not something we have the resources for."

"What about the clones?" said Kruger.

VanHoff waved a dismissive hand, "They're expendable. We already have what we need."

"Very well, then."

"Just one request, Commander Kruger. I would like, if at all possible, that Dr. Jann Malbec be taken alive. I have a bone to pick with her, and it would bring me no end of pleasure to do it face-to-face."

"Understood, sir."

11

SUBTERRANEAN

The colonists trapped in the biodome made several futile attempts to get the door open, ignoring the broadcasts by the Chinese that persistence in their attempts would be met with violence. After a time though, it became increasingly evident to them that it was just not going to happen. They were trapped, held captive inside their own biodome, with no way to access the larger facility save through the door to the connecting tunnel. So one by one they wandered away.

Jann contented herself by retiring to her old wicker chair on the central dais. Some of the other colonists had also gathered around, but their mood was somber and resigned.

"I am really getting sick of this shit," said Rachel, one of the few remaining original colonists. And who could blame her? Since landing on the planet, over a decade ago now, she had seen nothing but hardship and the constant attempts by others to manipulate and interfere with the very serious business of surviving in a hostile environment.

"You know, I had this naive idea once that things might get better," she continued.

"Yeah, I know how you feel. It would be real nice if they all just left us alone," said Steven, another long-suffering colonist.

"Isn't gonna happen. We're just too valuable to them," Rachel replied with a resigned sigh. "We're just a group of lab monkeys as far as they're concerned. They want us for what's inside us."

They went silent for a while before Steven spoke again. "So, what now? What have they got planned? What's going to happen to us?"

JANN COULDN'T TAKE this conversation anymore. It seemed to her that the colonists had resigned themselves to their fates and nothing she could say was going to change that. She rose from the wicker chair and went for a walk around the outer rim of the biodome. Gizmo followed beside her. After a short period of aimless meandering, Jann arrived at the place in the biodome wall where it opened out into a long tunnel. This was the fish farm. Next to it was another, similar tunnel, but this one was derelict, the roof structure had collapsed in on itself many years ago. There was still a door into it but it had been sealed up for a long time. This tunnel had originally been used for soil processing and had an airlock entrance out onto the planet's surface. But this process had long been relocated to the cave system that Nills had discovered beneath the colony itself. Jann stopped and stared at the sealed door for some time.

"Gizmo, can you access Colony One schematics or do you need to be connected to the main systems?"

"I have them stored locally so, yes, I can access them."

"Show me what you've got on this old tunnel."

Gizmo projected various schematics onto the wall beside Jann.

"Wait, this one here—can you zoom in a bit more on this?"

Jann looked at the exploded diagram of the soil processing tunnel as it would have been when it was in operation.

"Do you have any schematics of the cave system beneath the biodome?"

"Not as such, Jann. These are hidden places. There were no maps or drawings created of them. Remember, it was only discovered during the collapse of the original colony. Nills never made any schematic of it. However, I could replicate a reasonably accurate rendering from my own accumulated sensory data."

"Really, you can do that?"

"Of course. Let me show you."

With that the droid began to sketch out the cave

system. It took it less than a few seconds to complete it. "There, that is as much detail as I can access."

Jann looked at it for a moment, examining the curved organic structure that the droid had rendered. "Can you overlay the derelict tunnel onto this drawing, in the exact location it would be?"

"Sure."

Jann studied the resultant schematic at the point where the two intersected with each other for quite some time. "Can you zoom in on this section here, Gizmo?"

Jann pointed to an area on the diagram. "Wait. What's that?"

"That is an access point."

"You mean, there is a way down into the cave system from this tunnel?"

"Correct. I remember Nills discussing this access route. There is a 72.3% probability of it still functioning, assuming the tunnel has sufficient integrity to hold one atmosphere of pressure."

Jann looked at Gizmo. "Well, there's only one way to find out. I need you to go find Xenon. Don't tell anyone else what we're planning here. Just say I need him, and bring him here, okay?"

"Sure." Gizmo sped off through the dense vegetation of the biodome to seek out Xenon.

It didn't take long for them to return, and Jann had Gizmo project the schematics again for Xenon, so she could explain to him what her plan was.

"I think there may be a way to get out of here and

make contact with Colony Two. There's an access route from this old derelict tunnel into the subterranean cave system that is now used for soil processing."

"I see." Xenon scratched his chin. "But I don't understand how that can help us. There's nothing down there except some autonomous machines and an airlock out onto the surface that the soil harvesters use. There are sections that don't even have an atmosphere."

"Yes, I know." Jann lowered her voice. "But there is an area down there, a secret area, an area that the original Nills used to hide out when the colony was going to hell, during the first wave of infection. If I can get in there, it has the systems that will enable me to see what's going on in Colony One, and possibly contact Colony Two."

"A secret place?"

"It's a long story, Xenon. But trust me, it's there."

"I see. So how can I help?"

"Well, we need to open this door. Gizmo has run the numbers and calculated a high probability that the access point still functions. However, there may not be an atmosphere behind this door. So we'll need to edge it open slowly until it sucks in enough air from the biodome to equalize the pressure."

"It's worth a shot. But you're forgetting one thing." He looked up at the roof of the biodome and pointed. "This place is covered with cameras, see there's one over there." He pointed to a small opaque hemisphere attached to the superstructure of the roof. "They'll see everything we're trying to do."

"Then we need to take them out."

"How? They're too high up to reach."

"Leave it to me." With that Jann disappeared off through the vegetation. Over to where the hydroponics were arrayed in neat symmetrical rows. From one of the beds she pulled out half a dozen long, thin aluminum bars that had been used to support the growing plants. She brought them back to where Xenon and Gizmo were waiting.

Jann hefted one of the thin bars over her shoulder, took a step back, and launched it straight at the camera. It buried itself dead center, plastic shards falling onto the floor all around.

"Okay, that's one. Let's go find the others."

AFTER ABOUT HALF AN HOUR, Jann had managed to take out four cameras at different locations around the biodome. She also managed to acquire a number of other colonists who were keen to know what she was up to. She brought them back with her to the sealed door to the soil processing tunnel and outlined the plan. They also acquired a number of steel bars that they could use to help lever the door open against the one atmosphere of pressure inside the biodome.

Word spread around the captive colonists that Jann Malbec had a plan—hope had returned. But for some, it was not hope they saw, but recklessness. Exposing the biodome to the exterior environment could mean disaster. As a consequence, a crowd had gathered and far from acting as a cohesive unit, in their own best interest, they squabbled and bickered. Jann was now concerned that this would achieve nothing other than to attract the attention of their Asian overlords.

It was Xenon who finally managed to establish some rational thinking amongst the group. "We must try. Otherwise we are at the mercy of those who regard us as laboratory experiments. That future is not one that I wish to contemplate."

It was through this line of dialogue that order in the biodome was restored, even if it was somewhat reluctant. It was agreed that the bulk of the colonists would disperse and act as normal, whatever that meant within the constraints of the current situation. This left Jann, Xenon, Gizmo and around a half dozen others to wrestle with the door into the derelict tunnel. Gizmo, for its part, had calculated the probability of the area behind the door having integrity compatible with sustaining one atmosphere at approximately 67.54%. But, as the little robot was no longer connected to the main Colony One systems, this had been derived with greatly reduced computational power. Nonetheless, it was good enough for Jann.

She spun the locking wheel on the door. Xenon and a few others rammed a number of the steel bars into the doorjamb to act as levers.

"Okay, see if it will move." Jann stepped back.

A gap appeared as the colonists applied leverage, it

hissed with the sound of air escaping into the space behind.

"Keep it open, let it fill." Jann had now thrown her weight into the mix.

The hissing increased and the gap became larger. It grew in intensity as they applied more pressure. The colonists all groaned with the physical exertion expended to keep the door from slamming shut.

"How long do we need to keep this up?"

"Just keep it open."

"What if it doesn't stop?"

"Just shut up, and keep the pressure on."

After what seemed like an eternity of physical endurance, the hissing slowed. Jann smiled. "Listen, it's holding. Come on, push harder."

When it came, it was almost instant. The pressure equalized and the door swung open in one swift movement. Two of the colonists lost their balance and went sprawling across the floor. Gizmo switched on its floodlight and illuminated the long forgotten tunnel. Ahead they could see where the roof had collapsed. It was only around ten meters in. There was nothing else in the space save for dust and crumpled metal roof structure. But it held the pressure, the tons of Martian dirt overhead creating an effective seal.

"Gizmo, how far in is the access point?"

The little robot was already moving in through the tunnel. "Approximately two meters past that point." It pointed to where the collapsed roof structure met the floor.

"Dammit, we'll have to dig."

Fortunately the biodome was well stocked with tools for moving soil and before long Xenon had organized a team. They quickly worked their way forward through the tunnel. A spade clanged off the floor. "I think this is it." Xenon tapped the floor again as a hollow sound revealed the location of the long forgotten access point. Jann knew it would be similar to one in the module attached to the medlab. A flat, hinged, plate lying flush with the floor. They swept the dirt off it, and Xenon jammed the edge of the spade into the gap, and leaned on it. It cracked open enough for the others to grab it with their fingers and lift it up to reveal a dark hole descending into the Martian sub-surface. Gizmo shone its light down. They could see a ladder extending a short distance to the floor of a narrow tunnel.

"Do you think you can climb down there to check it out, Gizmo?"

With that the little droid grabbed the sides of the opening and lowered itself down, telescoping its arms as it went, then finally dropping onto the floor below. It moved its light slowly around the space and then disappeared off down a tunnel. They could hear it move around and, after a few minutes, it returned.

"There's another airlock up ahead that leads into the soil processing cave."

"Does it have an atmosphere?"

"Yes, it should."

"Okay, let's try it." Jann descended the ladder and looked down along the dark passage.

"I see it," she shouted up to Xenon and the others.

A trickle of dirt started to fall down into the opening and Jann looked up. "What's that?"

"The tunnel roof, it's becoming unstable. Quick you better get out of there now." Xenon was shouting down to her.

"No, we've come this far, I'm not going back."

More dirt fell in as the roof shifted, its enormous weight too much for the flimsy support the colonists had rigged up.

"Go..." Jann shouted at Xenon. "Get out... get out now."

The trickle of dirt turned into a cascade, then into a torrent and the space began to fill up at an alarming rate, forcing Jann and Gizmo to move farther along the passageway.

"Quick, Gizmo. Let's get this airlock open." Jann moved just as the tunnel roof finally collapsed in a tsunami of dust, and dirt, and darkness.

12

SANCTUM

Jann spat and coughed as grit filled her mouth. Darkness enveloped her. "Gizmo?"

She stood up and felt for the wall, or anything that would orient her. She heard Gizmo's motors whirr and turned to see a light emanating from the little robot's head, as it extracted itself from a mound of soil.

"Gizmo, are you okay?"

"I am 98.6% operational, excluding that fact that I have no external systems access."

Jann coughed again. "We need to get this airlock open, the air in here will run out soon." She spun the locking wheel and opened the door as a waft of stale air overpowered her nostrils.

"Ahh... what's that smell?"

"I am sorry, I can not offer any assistance in that regard as my olfactory sensors pale in comparison to the performance of the human apparatus."

GERALD M. KILBY

"Count yourself lucky you can't smell this." She held her nose.

They moved into the airlock and Jann spun the locking wheel on the outer door. A green light flashed on an alert panel.

"Okay, here goes." She tugged at the door.

"It's not moving." She put her foot against the wall and pulled. It refused to budge.

"Help me Gizmo, if we don't get this open I'll run out of breathable air."

"I estimate you have forty-two hours before you die."

"I really don't need to know that, Gizmo."

"My pleasure, I am here to assist."

Jann looked at the eccentric robot as it grabbed the door handle.

"Are you sure a rock didn't fall on your head and readjust your brain?"

"Quite sure, Jann. My brain is not in my head."

"Never mind. Let's push… one, two, three…"

The door moved a little. Buoyed by this achievement Jann redoubled her efforts and they finally created an opening wide enough for both Jann and Gizmo to pass through.

They entered a long narrow passageway. The air was fresher here, gone was the foul smell from the airlock. After around ten meters or so, it opened out into the main soil processing cave. This was where the colony extracted its water. Robotic harvesters fed the processing plant with soil acquired from outside. At the far end of

98

the cave, automatic airlocks facilitated the coming and going of these robots. Some fed the plant and some removed the spent soil back out onto the surface. None were moving when Jann and Gizmo entered. This was not unusual, as the reclamation and recycling system in Colony One was highly efficient. The plant only needed to top up the reservoir every so often, and since Martian soil contained a lot of H_2O, the process required only brief periods of activity for the harvesters.

They moved through the cave illuminated only by the light from the droid. Jann caught glimpses in the shadows of the slumbering harvesters, waiting patiently to be called into action by the colony systems. They passed by the main access route, a stairway leading up to a concourse near the operations area above. Jann could take this route but it would only lead her right slap bang in to the hornet's nest. If the Chinese were planning the defense of the colony then that area would be busy. Instead she was heading for the cave beneath the medlab. The same one that Nills had taken her to when he had rescued her and Paolio from the demented Decker, where she had first met Gizmo. This cave had been utilized by Nills and the other colonists as a refuge from the mayhem that raged through the original colony population. It was in there that he had carved out an operations center for clandestine surveillance. *It's the perfect place to... do what?* thought Jann. *What exactly am I going to do, even If I manage to get there?*

She put it out of her mind and concentrated on

finding the location of the access point. This was not an easy task, as it had been sealed up long ago. What was the point of having a secret place if anyone could find it and enter? And since the soil processing area was frequently visited by technicians maintaining the equipment, the access point would be well hidden.

"Gizmo, where are we?"

The little robot projected a 3D schematic into the space directly in front of them. It zoomed and rotated as Gizmo calculated the correct orientation. "This is us here," a red dot illuminated their position on the diagram, "...and that should be where the entrance is."

"Okay, let's keep going."

Gizmo led the way, as its sensors derived their position in space from a combination of ultrasonic and microwave frequencies. It was like a bat. It did not require light to know where it was or what surrounded it. It might not be able to smell as well as a human but it had many more useful tricks up its metallic sleeve.

"Here it is." The droid stopped and shone its light onto a bare cave wall.

"Where? I don't see anything."

"It is here, behind approximately one meter of regolith."

"Great, more digging." Jann started looking around for something to use as a tool.

"Wait," said Gizmo, "I have a better idea."

The droid went quiet for a moment, not moving, not

saying anything. Jann began to wonder if it had shut itself down. "Gizmo?"

Before it replied she heard the whirr of an electric motor starting up, and she spun around to locate its direction. Across the cave the sound grew louder, moving toward them. She stepped back, "Gizmo?"

Out of the gloom a harvester bot trundled across the floor.

"I thought one of these would be useful. After all this is what they are designed to do— dig."

"Gizmo, you are a genius."

"Yes, I know."

"But how did you do that? I thought you were denied access to the colony mainframe?"

"These are on a sub-system, low level stuff. I am able to access those sectors."

The harvester moved over to the cave wall and started to literally eat it. It began to churn up the hard compacted regolith and fill its hopper. Dust filled the air as it chewed into the wall, loose dirt piled up around it like crumbs from a mechanical feast. It worked at a furious pace, devouring everything in its path, both soil and rock fell equally to its mechanical jaws. It stopped with a loud wheeze, dust billowing up from its base, then reversed out of the gaping hole. Gizmo shone its light inside.

"There it is, just as I calculated."

"The only problem now is, how can we hide this? If someone were to come down here they would see it?"

"I can set the harvester to clear away the debris into the processing plant."

"We'll still need something to conceal the entrance. Even if it's just cosmetic. I don't think there's anything we can do that will pass a close examination."

Gizmo slowly swept the area with light, coming to a halt on a stack of storage containers.

"We could move these in front of the entrance, and pull them in closer once we are inside."

"Okay, let's get going then."

They moved fast to drag everything into position. Jann's main concern now was of being discovered. Any moment the door to the concourse area above could open and the game would be up. As it was, they were making one hell of a racket.

"Hurry, Gizmo." They squeezed in behind the container camouflage they had just assembled. Jann grabbed the locking wheel on the door and put all her weight behind it. It was stiff from the dirt that had penetrated the mechanism it had been entombed in for so long. But it moved. And after much grunting from Jann they finally entered the hidden space that she had repurposed for her experiments beneath the medlab.

"Quick, Gizmo, get the door shut. I'll see what's going on." She sat down at the monitors and flipped a number of switches to bring them online. Screens flickered to life as Jann tapped icons to display camera feeds from inside the colony. It was the same setup that Nills had used to monitor the whereabouts of the unfortunate ISA Commander Decker.

"Jann, my sensors have picked up activity in the soil processing area."

"What? They must have heard us, dammit." She tapped an icon to bring up a video feed. It was dark and grainy, but some illumination had entered the space from the direction of the stairs to the operations area.

"Look." Jann pointed to movement on the monitor. "It's the robot, Yutu. They must have sent it down to investigate."

The quadruped moved silently into the camera's field of view, then stopped, and its head slowly rotated.

"I do not like that robot," said Gizmo.

"What's it doing?"

"It is scanning the area for anomalies."

"Define anomaly—wait, it's stopped." The robot's head was pointing directly at the storage containers that Jann and Gizmo had just moved. It rose up on its four legs and started to move again. This time straight for the containers.

"Shit, it's coming over."

The robot moved slowly and purposefully, like a big cat stalking prey. It arrived at the location of the containers and started to move around the stack.

"Goddammit." Jann jumped up. "Quick find something we can jam into the door handle, anything."

Gizmo picked up a long steel rod. "This might do."

Jann grabbed it and raced for the door. But before she could reach it the ground shook with the force of an explosion somewhere up above and the cave was plunged into total darkness.

"What the hell?"

13

BATTLE

Emergency lighting flickered on inside the cave as Jann's brain tried to make sense of what had just happened. It took her a moment to reorient herself.

"The main power source has shut down. The facility is now operating on backup power." Gizmo was at the console, seemingly trying to reconnect with the broader colony systems. Jann stood motionless, her senses on high alert. She realized she was still holding the steel bar. "The robot, Yutu, is it still there?" she said as she moved to wedge it into the door's locking mechanism.

"I have no feed, minimal systems operational."

"Life support? Do we still have life support?"

"Affirmative... backup systems coming online now."

The monitors started to flicker back to life as Jann returned to the desk. "What the hell is going on?"

"The facility still has full structural integrity. No loss of pressure."

"That explosion came from outside."

Jann's fingers danced across the screens, tapping icons, bringing up video feeds. "Biodome looks intact." She could make out groups of startled colonists looking around, clutching each other, they were frightened. She scanned the faces and spotted Xenon. *At least he got out before the tunnel roof collapsed,* she thought.

Another feed flickered to life, showing the operations room above; several of the Xaing Zu crew worked the systems at a frenetic pace. They too were trying to figure out what was going on. "Look." Jann pointed at the screen. "It's Yutu. The robot must have been ordered back."

"I do not like that robot," said Gizmo again.

"Gizmo, snap out of it... talk to me... comms, anything on comms?"

"Nothing. But my calculations put the explosion at fifty meters due south of the facility. Near the location of the main reactor. They probably targeted the main power line."

Jann sat back and watched the monitors for a few minutes, trying to divine some meaning from the images. She located two of the Chinese in the operations room, along with Yutu. Two more were outside the biodome door, and armed. That left... how many? She wasn't sure if all of them were in the facility or if some had been sequestered back on their ship.

"I am picking up a transmit," said Gizmo, as radio static hissed out from the comm speaker. Jann could see that the Chinese in the operations room were also getting it, their body language changed suddenly.

"This is Commander Kruger, of the Colony One Mars Consortium. You have failed to comply with our request to vacate our facility." The metallic voice broke through the hiss of static, the sandstorm raging outside causing the signal to break up. *"...last chance... leave now..."* Then it went dead.

"Xaing Zu are up to something. Look." Jann pointed at the monitor of the operations room. The Chinese were putting on their EVA suits. "Are they planning to go outside, in this storm?"

"It could also be that COM are coming in."

"But why EVA suits, then?"

"Because they fear a loss of pressure."

Jann looked over at Gizmo. "You mean, if they don't leave then COM are going to open a hole in the facility—oh shit."

"Indeed," said Gizmo. "For what it is worth you are relatively safe here, as this section is sealed and isolated from the main structure."

"But what about the biodome, the colonists? This will be a disaster—the end of Colony One—we have to do something." Jann jumped up from her seat and started pacing. "This is nuts, they'll destroy everything that's taken over a decade to establish—and for what? So they can simply repossess it?"

"Activity on the surface around the perimeter." Gizmo jolted Jann back to the immediate situation by projecting a holographic image of the Colony One facility onto a small holo-table. It stuttered and fizzed as it rendered.

"The storm is interfering with the sensors."

Nonetheless, they could clearly see two dots approaching the colony from the northern side.

"There, look, what's that?" Jann pointed at the dots.

"COM rovers approaching, judging by the speed."

"Do we have any cameras working on the outside?"

The monitors flickered through a series of blurry images of dust and sand. They failed to penetrate the swirling maelstrom, serving only to show a few meters of visibility and rendering a vague outline of the exterior of the colony. But it was enough to make out a new addition to the infrastructure. On the roof of one of the airlocks, a bulky pulsed energy weapon had been mounted. It was squat, not unlike a standard artillery piece. As Jann studied the structure she could see a suited figure operating it, moving the weapon, aiming it at something.

"Are they're preparing to fire that weapon?"

But before Gizmo could reply another explosion rocked the cave, dust rained down on Jann, the power flickered off, and all went dark again.

"Shit. What was that?" Jann tried to orient herself in the pitch black of the cave before Gizmo flicked on its lights. The little robot moved back to the operations desk and started to investigate, interrogating and probing what colony systems still remained operational. A few seconds later auxiliary power came back online.

"The airlock in sector two has been compromised... loss of atmosphere in sector one... extensive damage."

"Shit, COM must have taken out that weapon before Xaing Zu could fire it."

"Still losing atmosphere in that sector... rate slowing..."

"The biodome?"

"Integrity at one hundred percent, still one atmosphere."

The monitors flicked back on again and the holograph of the facility ballooned back to life. They could see the advancing dots had reached within a few meters of the facility. From the exterior cameras that still worked, several COM mercenaries disgorged themselves from the vehicles—all heavily armed.

"Good god, it's a full scale invasion." Jann pointed at the armed figures entering via a damaged airlock. They now had access to a section of the facility with no atmosphere. Jann wondered how this was going to help them take over but then she realized they were sealing it up behind them. Once finished they would be able to enter the rest of the colony, without any loss of integrity. She struggled with her desire to do something— anything. Maybe she could get the colonists out of the biodome, hide them all down here. But that was pointless, the access route had caved in and even if she did manage to get them all in here, then what?

Another blast rocked the cave. This time it was an internal door being blown open. From the monitors Jann could see a firefight starting. COM had entered, the Chinese were firing weapons to try and repel the invasion. She could see two already down, injured or dead. The air was thick with dust from the blast and it bloomed with incandescent flashes from the pulse weapons. All she could do was stand and watch as the fate of Colony One was decided, once again, by violence.

14

CONTROL

Peter VanHoff watched the battle for Colony One unfold from the relative comfort of the COM Mars lander. In the end it had gone exactly to plan, although it would have been better had Xaing Zu just vacated the facility. But, they had decided to make a stand. He admired them for that, even if it was a futile exercise. He assumed it had more to do with saving face than any real consideration of military superiority.

It had taken less than twenty minutes from the moment Commander Kruger had given the command until the facility was secured, and his people in control. Kruger had sent him the *all clear* so now it was time for VanHoff to finally set foot in the very facility where the Janus bacteria had been created. His hope, his wish, his deepest desire, was that it still existed either in the facility or within the biology of the clone subject Langthorp. Time to find out. He rose from operations and signaled to the two remaining COM crew. "The facility is secure and a rover is on its way to pick us up. Bring the clone to the airlock, I will meet you down there. And make sure he's sedated for the trip."

THEY ENCASED Nills in an ill-fitting EVA suit so that he could be transported over to the medlab in Colony One. VanHoff and his genetics team needed him alive, at least for the moment. Nills was now strapped into a seat in the rover, his head bobbing and rocking as the rover bounced along the planet's surface. Outside, dust and sand whipped up all around, visibility was poor and the driver operated by means of a heads-up display rendered on the rover windshield. The journey was mercifully short and soon VanHoff could make out the lights atop of the Colony One biodome penetrating the dust. The rover came to a halt outside the main airlock, time to EVA. This was not a procedure that VanHoff relished. Far from it. Being cocooned inside bulky life support brought on a rising panic inside him. He fought to control it. It was only a few meters to the colony entrance, surely he could make that. Yet, what this situation did highlight in his mind was just how much Malbec had corrupted his ambition. He could be back home, in the warm and comforting environment of Earth, free from the debilitating curse of accelerated aging, enjoying life. But no, here he was, having to travel 200 million kilometers to this hellhole of a planet. He steeled himself and stepped out of the rover onto the surface of Mars.

From just inside the airlock Commander Kruger beckoned to him with a free arm, gesturing encouragement to move. VanHoff focused on the figure of the commander, and excluded all other exterior stimuli. It worked, he inched his way forward and into the airlock. A few moments later he removed his helmet and tried to calm his breathing.

"Are you okay?" The commander gave him a concerned look.

"I'm fine... fine." He composed himself for a moment before removing the bulky EVA suit.

By the time he arrived at the operations room in Colony One, the commander had brought him up to speed on the current status. He found it hard to focus on what Kruger was saying, as he kept looking around. It was hard to believe he was actually here, in the very place that had occupied his every waking moment for years. He sat down at the central table and surveyed the subdued figure of Jing Tzu, Xaing Zu Industries commander. His hands were bound behind his back, his head bowed in defeat.

"You should have left when you had the chance."

Jing Tzu lifted his head up slowly and glared at VanHoff.

"It seems two of your crew are dead. A high price to pay for naught."

VanHoff then turned to the commander. "What is your plan for them?"

"Fortunately, our Asian friends had the bright idea of incarcerating the current colonist population in the biodome. So I think we'll just throw them inside and see how they get on."

"Excellent. I trust you'll keep their hands tied before you cast them to the lions, it should make for good entertainment."

Jing Tzu was lifted out of his seat by two COM mercenaries, and dragged off to face an uncertain fate inside the biodome.

VanHoff now surveyed the monitors arrayed around the operations room. He was particularly interested in the video feed from the biodome, and could see clusters of colonists gathered together in various sectors. But there was one member of the colony population he was most interested in.

"Commander Kruger."

"Yes, sir."

"Before you deal with the Chinese, I want you to take a team, enter the biodome and find me Dr. Jann Malbec. Bring her to me—alive, if possible. I'll be in the medlab getting things set up."

"Yes sir."

BY THE TIME VanHoff reached the medlab he was beginning to feel an increasing sense of confidence in the mission. They had successfully taken back control of both facilities, and the situation was now completely under COM control. What's more, they had not sustained a single casualty. Now he was finally ready to get started on the main phase of the operation—to find the source of the Janus bacteria.

Already his team had moved the clone subject, Langthorp, onto the operating table in the medlab, where he lay sedated until they were ready. His genetics team were also in the process of moving in the new equipment that they had brought with them. VanHoff cast an eye around the medlab space. It was well set up, much better that he had anticipated. He did a cursory audit of its equipment as he moved from area to area. Finally he came to a sealed door. It was currently locked, access was via a keypad on the side. He peered in through the small window at its interior. It had been fashioned from one of the original landers, its circular interior was lined with units not unlike rows of safety deposit boxes in a bank vault. He looked back at the keypad and made a mental note to have his team get this door open.

It was some time later when his work in the medlab was disrupted by Kruger entering. He bore a concerned look, not something VanHoff wanted to see. The commander signaled to him to follow him outside. VanHoff obliged.

When they were out of earshot of the other crewmembers Kruger spoke. "We have not located Dr.

Malbec yet. She's not in the biodome and the colonists either don't know where she is or are not saying."

VanHoff stood silent for a moment. "This is a finite space. There are few places for someone to hide, she has to be here somewhere. And I want that woman found —now."

"Yes sir, she will be found."

"Wait a minute." VanHoff stroked his chin again. "I have a better idea. Come, follow me. We're going to talk to these colonists again. They know where she is, so let's not waste any more time pussyfooting around."

VanHoff and the commander were flanked by four well-armed COM mercenaries as the inner door to the biodome swung open. Inside, a knot of colonists were backing away as they advanced.

"You," shouted VanHoff at a frightened looking colonist. "Over here."

One of the mercenaries marched over, and grabbed her by the arm. "You heard the man." He dragged her over to where VanHoff and the others were standing, and kicked her in the back of the knees. She dropped down on the floor, frightened and shaking.

VanHoff turned to Kruger and pointed to a stubby pulsed weapon he had tucked inside a holster around his shoulder.

"Mind if I borrow that for a moment?"

Kruger unclipped the weapon and handed it to him.

VanHoff then moved to the kneeling colonist and placed a gentle hand on her head. "What's your name?"

"M... Ma... Maria."

"Well, Maria. Here's how you can help us. I want to know where Dr. Jann Malbec is." He stepped back and pointed the gun directly at her forehead.

"You've got ten seconds. Nine... eight... seven..."

15

ROCK

Jann watched the events in the biodome unfold with a deep sense of dread, mixed with an equal measure of helplessness. The very fabric of the colony was being eviscerated before her eyes, and what was she doing? Hiding. She was doing what she always did—run and hide. Like when she was a child. At the first sign of trouble she would take off across the fields and disappear into her secret place, where the world couldn't touch her, where her dreams were still tinged with hope. And here she was again, but this time there was no way out. Like a dystopian deja vu. The same, but worse.

The video feed showed Nills, unconscious on the medlab operating table. His chest rose and fell with each breath. Her hand reached out to touch the monitor, as if the action would make the reality... less painful. She had failed him. As she had failed the other colonists. They had placed their trust in her and now she had deserted them—run away. Now they knew the true Dr. Jann Malbec.

Her eyes moved from the prostrate form of Nills to the man standing over him. She knew that face. It was not one that you could easily forget. Old and haggard, limp fragile skin hung on brittle bones. It was Peter VanHoff. She could feel the cruelty radiate out from his being, even down here, under all this rock. His head moved, and for a brief second he looked straight at the camera. Jann recoiled and drew in a sharp breath.

"Holy crap, can he see us?"

"No, this is not possible," replied Gizmo.

She stood up, walked away from the monitors and sat down again on a low seat against the cave wall. Jann put her head in her hands.

"I hate this place. I hate the dust, and the sand. I hate the constant fight for survival. I hate the naiveté of these clones. I hate the need to run and hide all the time. I just want to go home. Back to Earth. Away from this madness."

"The probability of you returning to Earth is slim to none."

"I know, I know. I am destined to be trapped here... in this cave. Watching Nills die slowly on the monitor—and there's not a damn thing I can do about it. This is what it has come to... this is my fate."

"These events you speak of are yet to happen. And they are just one path of many possible outcomes. For it to come to pass a great many possibilities must line up in the correct sequence. Any disruption to that path, any deviation, no matter how small, will bring a different outcome."

Jann took her head out of her hands and looked over at Gizmo. "What the hell... does any of that mean?"

"It means there are a great many ways that this can play out. Your premonition of Nills' demise is just one possibility."

"I think you have finally lost it, Gizmo. I'm pretty sure something hard must have fallen on your head. You're not making any sense to me."

"What I am saying is, one rock can change the course of a river, if that rock is carefully placed. It will gather to it silt and sand and over time the river is moved."

"Where are you getting all this... philosophy from? What happened to *probabilities* and *analysis*?"

"I have been researching the writings of Confucius, to gain a better understanding of our Chinese guests."

Jann stood up. "I think I prefer Gizmo the analyst to Gizmo the philosopher. Finding a rock is not going to help us much." She looked over at the video feed from the medlab, and the unconscious figure of Nills. "What are they doing to him?"

"It is the Janus bacteria that they ultimately seek. Nills must be important in that search."

"We need to do something, we can't leave him there, at the mercy of these bastards."

"What do you suggest?"

"We can access the medlab from here so we wait until it's vacated, then sneak in and take him down here."

"Deja vu." said Gizmo. "I have been here before, with Nills, at this same operations desk as he discussed rescuing you from the psychotic Commander Decker."

Jann sat down and sighed. "But what would be the point of moving him? As soon as he was discovered missing they would rip the place apart and find us. We would only be buying time at best, giving ourselves away at worst." She sighed again, stood up and walked back across the cave.

"This is hopeless. There's no way out. They have us completely under their control and it's only a matter of time before they find us down here." She sat down and put her head in her hands again. "I've failed everyone, Nills, the colonists—there's no escaping it." She sat there in silence for quite some time, considering the hopelessness of her situation.

"Jann, you might want to see this."

She looked over at the robot, "What is it?"

"Activity in the biodome."

On the feed Jann could see Peter VanHoff holding a weapon to the head of one of the colonists. She was shaking uncontrollably, all the time pleading with them.

"Can we hear what's going on?"

"No, we have no audio feed."

"Damn, what's she saying?"

"She is telling them... that you are hiding out."

"Are you sure? How do you know that?"

"I can lip read, obviously."

Jann spun around, her hand over her mouth. "Shit, shit, shit. They'll find us."

"Wait... she is saying... you are in Colony Two." Gizmo looked over at Jann.

Jann stood silent for a while. "Are they buying it?"

They watched as VanHoff lowered the weapon, and handed it back to one of the mercenaries.

"Yes, he is not shooting the colonist Maria in the head."

"Well, we've bought some time, nothing more. They'll soon find out I'm not there and VanHoff won't give up trying to find me. I'm a loose end, and he doesn't strike me as a person who likes loose ends."

The mercenaries started to move out of the biodome, but before the door shut, the four remaining Chinese taikonauts were unceremoniously shoved inside. They stood with their backs to the door, hands bound behind them. The colonists gathered around, closing in on them.

"This could get nasty," said Jann, leaning her hand on the table as she peered closer at the monitor. "What are they saying, Gizmo?"

"Bastards... scumbags... let's tear them a new asshole..." Gizmo looked over at Jann.

She pointed back at the monitor. "Xenon, what's he saying?" He had stepped between and was appealing to the angry mob.

"Not enemy now... COM are the fight... don't waste energy on these scum..." His appeals seemed to be having the desired effect. Their body language changed, the moment passed, but not before the taikonauts were pelted with rotten fruit. Xenon raised a hand, the rain of fruit stopped. After some time the colonists dispersed. The Chinese simply sat down on the floor and nursed their bruised and battered egos.

Jann sat and watched until it was clear the mood in the biodome had settled down. She sighed and looked around at the cave as if it might prompt some solution to her dilemma. She had time, but not much else, and even that was limited. Nills was incarcerated in the medlab, soon to be under the scalpel, no doubt. She could do nothing for him, just watch as he was slowly dissected by the COM geneticists, probing his biology in their quest to unlock the secrets of the Janus bacteria.

Jann looked across the cave and her eyes came to rest on the incubator where the last remaining sample of that bacteria still existed. She walked over to it and peered in through the observation window as she placed a hand on its glass. She stood there motionless, just looking at it for some time.

"Gizmo," she finally said.

"Yes, Jann."

She looked back at the robot. "I think we may have found our *rock*."

"What do you mean?"

Jann looked back through the window at the petri dish. "This is what they came here for."

"Are you going to destroy it? You still have some time."

"No, Gizmo. I'm going to give it to them."

The droid moved over to where Jann stood and looked in through the window. "Is that wise?"

"It depends on the manner in which it is given."

"Now it is you that sounds like an ancient philosopher. I hate to admit it but I am confused."

Jann stood back from the incubator and turned to Gizmo. "I'm not going to hand it to them, Gizmo. I'm going to release it to the environment."

The robot was silent for a moment as it analyzed the ramifications of this strategy. "That would be more that just throwing a *rock* in the river. That would be a very large boulder."

Jann turned back to the incubator. "The colonists are all immune to it, but the others..." Her sentence trailed off.

"It may give us an edge."

"The repercussions of its release into the general environment are difficult to predict, Jann. Too much random chaos in the equation to enable any reliable analysis."

"Chaos is our ally. If past performance is anything to go by, then by morning, they should all be fighting each other. My only concern is the taikonauts in the biodome. They could put the colonists at risk."

"Their hands are bound, that would reduce the risk somewhat."

Jann's hand moved to the console on the incubator, her finger hovered over the button marked *open*.

She hesitated.

"Why have you stopped?"

"Before I do this, there is a greater concern that needs to be considered."

"What is that?"

"None of them can ever be allowed to return to Earth." She looked at Gizmo for a moment, then hit the button.

There was a faint hiss as the front of the incubator cracked open and slowly rose up. Jann reached in and took the petri dish in her hand. "Well, here goes." She opened the lid, exposing the bacteria to the environment.

For a moment, she stood still, looking at the splattered agar gel. Perhaps she expected more to happen, a more dramatic moment to herald the enormity of what she had just done. But there was none. Just silence.

"What would be the most efficient way to have the bacteria permeate the facility, Gizmo?"

"I would suggest waiting until the colony is asleep. Then access the medlab and place the dish in there, into an air recycling vent."

"Then let's do that." Jann checked the time. "Another hour or so and we should be ready to go."

. . .

DARKNESS FALLS QUICKLY ON MARS. The transition from day to night is abrupt. As the sun sinks below the horizon so too does the light. Mars possesses insufficient atmosphere to soften the blow with a dusky prelude. So, Jann and Gizmo had not long to wait for the inhabitants of Colony One to settle into the nighttime ritual of preparing for sleep. She had worried that some of the COM mercenaries, and maybe even VanHoff, would go back to their ship for the night. But that was not the case. Jann watched as VanHoff made preparation to retire to one of the bigger accommodation pods. She gave it a few more hours before she and Gizmo took the short tunnel to the medlab access point. It was the same tunnel that Gizmo had carried the stricken ISA medical doctor Paolio, when Nills had rescued her. Now, it seemed it was almost time to return the favor.

Gizmo slipped out of the airlock and up the ramp, its tracked wheels making barely a sound. Jann followed and entered the code into the keypad to open the door into the medlab proper. It was dim, with just spots of localized light around some of the workbenches. She walked over to where Nills lay and checked the monitor. His vitals were good, if somewhat elevated. She could just make out his face in the dull reflected green light from the screens. He looked pained. While Jann checked Nills, Gizmo unscrewed a grill from an air vent on the back wall of the medlab. It then placed the petri dish with the exposed bacteria inside and replaced the panel. It would be sucked through the recyclers and then redistributed to all areas of Colony One. Gizmo had estimated approximately 1.34 hours for full environmental contamination.

Jann breathed a sigh of relief as they moved back down through the connecting tunnel, although it pained her terribly to leave Nills behind. But by morning, the bacteria would be starting to work on the physiology of those who had no immunity to it. Some would go the way of Commander Decker, turning into deranged killers. Others would end up being the victims. Jann was counting on it.

16

TAIKONAUT DOWN

Xenon shifted his position, for possibly the hundredth time, on the bed of leaves he had fashioned in the hope that he might find a more comfortable arrangement. It was a futile exercise, made bearable only by the onset of extreme fatigue. But now that the Martian dawn was starting to filter through the semi-transparent biodome membrane, his body clock was no longer cooperating with his need for sleep. He was contemplating returning to his back as he began to feel the hard floor of the biodome dig into his pelvis, when a sharp, loud shriek reverberated around the cavernous space. He sat up and listened. Others had also heard it. Heads and bodies popped up through the vegetation all around him, like prairie dogs on alert.

"Did you hear that?" Rachel asked in a whisper from her position wedged between the bases of two banana trees.

Before Xenon had a chance to utter a response another shriek pierced the dawn silence. It was louder this time and was followed by the sound of running—getting closer and louder, until finally a frenzied Xaing Zu taikonaut burst through the vegetation heading straight for Xenon. Fortunately, his hands were still tied behind his back so his gait was ragged and unbalanced. Xenon dove for his legs as he passed and took him down swiftly. The other colonists, observing this spectacle, emerged from the surrounding foliage and pounced on the hapless runner.

Even though he was pinned down beneath several colonists he still put up a frenzied fight, kicking and screaming in Mandarin, a language none of them understood. Not that they needed to. It was clearly evident that he was totally demented. Two other Chinese crew came panting onto the scene, both had their hands still bound. They stopped and bent over as they tried to catch a breath, now that their crazy runaway friend had been halted and contained.

"What the hell is up with him?" Xenon looked over at the Chinese as they slowly regained the ability to breathe enough to speak.

"Crazy bastard... started bashing his head on the floor, then ran off."

Xenon stood up, once he was sure that the others had a good grip on the distraught captive. He still kicked and bucked with demonic strength. "Rachel, go find something to tie him up with. He'll just injure himself more if we don't."

Xenon reached down to where he had been lying earlier, picked up his knife and unsheathed it. He turned to the Chinese commander, Jing Tzu, who backed off as Xenon approached.

"You came here thinking we are all just lab rats, to be experimented on, to be disposed of, as a means to an end."

"Some did, yes, this is true, I will not lie."

"It was your mission."

"Not mine. You have my word on that, not mine."

"Then what was your mission?"

"As commander... to keep everybody safe... as best I can."

Xenon looked down at the still struggling crewmember, then back at the commander. "Well, you failed, didn't you?"

The commander lowered his head.

"Yes, I failed."

Xenon hefted the knife in his hand, grabbed the commander by the arm—and cut his bonds.

"We are not animals."

Jing Tzu nodded his thanks as Xenon freed the others. They rubbed their wrists and arms as they tried to get some feeling back. Jing Tzu knelt down beside his stricken colleague and snapped at him in Mandarin. But the response was muted as the deranged crewmember had finally run out of steam. His eyes rolled in his head and he stopped fighting.

"I don't understand what happened to him. Dan Ma is one of our most competent taikonauts. That's why he was chosen for this mission."

"He needs medical help," said Xenon.

"Do you have any idea what caused him to go crazy like that?" Jing Tzu gestured down at his comrade.

"It's just Mars. It can send some people demented. Too much for them, I suppose." Xenon looked at him and shook his head. "Pick him up and follow me."

They took him into one of the food processing pods, off the main biodome, and laid him out on a bench. "You all stay locked up in here and keep an eye on him. That's the deal. Otherwise we tie you up again."

Jing Tzu gave a reluctant nod. What choice did he have?

Xenon retreated with Rachel and the other colonists to the central dais of the biodome. They were all clearly agitated by the morning's events.

"Could it be happening again, you know, like the stories about how the first colony went crazy?"

Xenon scratched his chin. "That was a long time ago, Rachel. All in the past."

"He needs medical help," she said. "And we need to get out of here. What are these COM guys playing at, they can't keep us in here forever."

"No, they can't. Soon things will start needing

maintenance. The colony can't run unless they let us out." Xenon lifted his head up. "I have an idea. Maybe this is an opportunity to get COM in here."

"How?"

"I'm going to write them a message."

"I can't see how that's going to work."

"It all depends on what you say. So let's find something to make a sign with."

Ten minutes later Xenon was standing in front of one of the working cameras monitoring the biodome. He held a sign aloft, cobbled together from the side of a food storage crate.

KRUGER SIPPED on a coffee and surveyed his surroundings. He was sitting in an old battered armchair in an area the colonists referred to as *the common room*. What struck him most was the shabbiness of it all. The walls were scuffed and yellowing. The furniture, if you could call it that, was made from materials scavenged from a scrapheap, albeit a space age one. It was in deep contrast to the elegant gleam of their own spacecraft. He had seen this sort of place before. It reminded him of asteroid mines where there seemed to be this visceral need for the miners to deconstruct anything resembling a clean modern environment into a post apocalyptic interior. He hated those places. To him they stank of discord and disorder. As if the natural order of the universe towards entropy had been allowed free reign. The descent into chaos aided by humanity rather than met head on and overcome. His job was to see order maintained at all times. Now that the primary mission objectives of securing control of both colony facilities had been achieved, he needed to get control of the colonists. The hardware was secure, time to deal with the wetware.

VanHoff and his team of geneticists were now free to pursue their mission. That left him to manage the transition to COM control as he saw fit. That was his job, and he was damn good at it. He was helped, of course, by the fact that he enjoyed it. He relished the thought of returning this place to the gleaming white modern citadel that it ought to be. In fact, he couldn't wait to get started. But first it was time to take stock. He refilled his coffee cup and started on a mental inventory.

First was an assessment of human resources. One crewmember was stationed on the landing craft. There she would stay. In the event that they needed to run away fast, the ship would be ready to take off. Three others were stationed in Colony Two along with one of the geneticists. Kruger considered that this was a little under resourced, he would have preferred twice that for comfort. But making do with limited resources was the hallmark of space travel. These would be sufficient, as long as the colonists remained subdued. That left five in Colony One, excluding VanHoff and the other geneticist, Dr. Molotov. A totally inadequate number. There was no question in Kruger's mind, he would need to get the colonists on board with the reality of the new hegemony —the sooner the better. Things needed to be maintained, managed, processed. The great engine that was Colony One needed care and attention to support the survival of all it contained. The colonists would come around. They would move on and accept the realities given time. And the best way to do that was to deal with the leaders first. Cut off the head, so to speak.

Before leaving Earth, Kruger had done his research. In military terms the colonists had already proved their mettle by dispensing with Dr. Vanji and his collaborators. Then they had to deal with internal insurrection. No mean feat for a ragtag bunch of subhumans. It took leadership to achieve these victories. And if the transition back to COM control was to go smoothly then this very same leadership needed to be quashed. Nills Langthorp, the clone, had already been subdued. VanHoff had him locked down and ready to go under the knife in his quest to discover the biological voodoo that Dr. Vanji had engineered here. Kruger felt a twinge of sorrow for the clone. *Poor bastard,* he thought. To die in battle was one thing, but to be dissected to death was a gruesome end to such a leader. But this was not Kruger's department. VanHoff, and COM, wrote his paycheck, so they got to call the shots. His job was to execute the mission, secure the facilities and ensure a smooth transition of power.

So the clone was ticked off Kruger's mental list. Next was Xenon, the weird Hybrid, the last of his species. A shiver ran up Kruger's spine as he thought of what this person represented. VanHoff and his crew regarded him as a very precious individual, not because of any great intellectual prowess but because he represented, in their eyes, the very pinnacle of their craft. To Kruger, though, he was just another weird biological product from the genetic horror show that was Colony Mars. But still, he would be easy to deal with. As it was, he was securely incarcerated along with the others in the biodome. But this was a situation that could not be sustained for much longer. It was a fortunate stroke of luck that the Chinese had herded them all in there, for their own safety. It made his task of taking the facility much more of a direct military confrontation, without the risk of civilian casualties. The Chinese had paid the price for their concern, now they too were locked up tight.

So Xenon was also accounted for. He would be the one that Kruger would need to get on board and show the reality of the new situation. They would have a chat and the colonists would be released from the biodome, back to work—and life would go on. But time enough for that, he would let them stew for a while longer. Then their freedom would taste so much sweeter. Less incentive for agitation, lest their freedoms be taken away again.

That left Dr. Jann Malbec, a loose end in his plan, a box that Kruger could not yet tick. He refilled his coffee cup one more time and considered this enigma. *Where the hell is she?* There were only so many places that you could hide out on Mars. It's not like she could head for the hills, hole up in some cave, living off the land. She had to be in one of the colonies. His crew in Colony Two had not reported back yet, which suggested they had nothing to report, which suggested they had not found her. But the longer this went on the more of an enigma it posed for him. What's more, VanHoff was getting increasingly agitated by the lack of closure. It seemed to Kruger that VanHoff had a deep systemic hatred of her. In his mind she was the single individual responsible for the destruction of his dream. Kruger could see his point. If he was locked inside the disintegrating body that VanHoff possessed then he too would be pretty pissed off, if the cure he had spent so much time and resources on was taken from him. Particularly by a rookie astronaut with a moral conscience. Seriously pissed off.

Yet she was not to be underestimated. She had proved herself thus far. The only surviving member of the ill-fated ISA mission. And she had elevated herself to an almost spiritual reverence within the colonist psyche. Those sorts of leaders were always the most formidable. They had a way of really screwing up the plan. She needed to be found and fast.

His earpiece chimed. "Commander, you'd better come in to operations and take a look at this."

"What is it?"

"Best you just take a look."

Kruger downed the dregs of his now cold coffee with a grimace and stood up. He picked up the PEP weapon that he had laid on the table while having breakfast, looped it over his shoulders and headed out.

. . .

"HOW LONG HAS this been going on?" Kruger was looking at a video feed from the biodome.

"Just started, sir. Five minutes, tops."

The main monitor showed a number of colonists gathered around Xenon. He was holding a makeshift sign. It said, *URGENT. Medical assistance needed!*

"Hmmm." Kruger rubbed the corners of his mouth with the thumb and index finger of his right hand, as if this gesture would somehow coax his brain into a better understanding of what the problem might be. Nothing came to mind. But it did present an opportunity to start talking turkey with the Hybrid.

"Come on, follow me. Let's go find what the hell they're up to."

COMMANDER KRUGER, flanked by two other COM crew stood inside the short biodome entrance tunnel. Their weapons were drawn, taking no chances. At the far end stood Xenon. Beside him some colonists were carrying what looked to be an unconscious Xaing Zu taikonaut.

"He needs help." Xenon gestured at the comatose figure. "Medical help."

"Yeah? What's his problem?"

"He went crazy, started bashing his head on the floor, then we tied him up, for his own safety."

Kruger sighed and turned to his team. "You two get a hold of him and drag him in to the medlab."

"Yes sir."

"And you," he pointed the business end of a PEP weapon at Xenon. "You're coming with me. We need to talk."

17

HAPPENING AGAIN

Peter VanHoff awoke with a headache. Not a bad one, as such. But he felt it had the potential to develop into something far more debilitating, given time. It was still roaming around the foothills of his frontal lobes an hour later when he finally made it to the medlab. He was anxious to get started on a series of experiments he and his team of geneticists had planned for the clone. So he was not amused when two COM mercenaries barged in carrying a comatose Xaing Zu taikonaut.

"The commander said we were to bring him in here. He needs some medical attention."

VanHoff looked up from his notes. "I would suggest putting him in an airlock without an EVA suit, and opening the outer door."

"The mercenaries looked from one to the other as they seriously considered this option.

"Wait." Dr. Alexi Molotov, geneticist and chief medical officer assigned to the mission, looked up from his microscope. "What's the matter with him?"

"I think he bashed his head on something."

Dr. Molotov came over and shone a light in the taikonaut's eyes. "Looks like concussion all right. Put him on that bed. I'll take a look at him."

The mercenaries did as ordered.

"Don't waste your time with him, Alexi." VanHoff's headache was getting worse.

"I'll just give him a quick scan. Make sure he hasn't fractured his skull."

"That makes you responsible for him."

"Understood."

"Just make sure you strap him down. We don't want him waking up and going kamikaze on us."

"He's Chinese, not Japanese."

"You know what I mean." VanHoff went back to his notes as the doctor started his tests on the taikonaut.

Playing nursemaid to the very people that tried to prevent him from taking over what was rightfully his was not what he wanted his team to be doing. But Dr. Molotov was not the type of individual he could just order around. He was one of the best geneticists money could buy. Sure, there were better ones. But VanHoff needed someone who was prepared to travel to Mars. Such a commute to work narrowed down the pool of available candidates considerably. But Dr. Molotov was not simply taking the job just for the money. He was also trying to make his name and saw this mission as a way of doing just that. Nevertheless, he would not be pushed into doing something he didn't want to. So VanHoff gritted his teeth and let the doctor indulge his Hippocratic conscience. For VanHoff the end always justified the means. And if Dr. Molotov's desire to provide humanitarian aid to the vanquished kept him content then so be it. He let him get on with it.

But there were more pressing matters. The ultimate objective of the mission was to piece together, from the scattered fragments of the genetically engineered biology of the colonists, the secret that enabled them to regenerate and repair their physiology. This was the end goal. Since the original source bacteria was now all but destroyed, as far as VanHoff was aware, then the only way left was for him and his team to forensically piece it together from whatever clues they could uncover. This needed to be planned and Dr. Molotov was getting himself sidetracked. Not a good start.

Yet VanHoff was glad of this distraction in a way, as his rumbling headache was not conducive to doing the complex cognitive gymnastics required for genetic reverse engineering. He rubbed his temples, popped another painkiller and sighed. There wasn't much he could do here at present so he decided to find commander Kruger and get an update on the search for the elusive Dr. Jann Malbec. Although the mere thought of her made his head throb even more. He headed out of the medlab as Dr. Molotov was applying a bandage to the injured taikonaut. He left him to it.

VanHoff had assumed that Malbec would be located by now. In fact he assumed she would be dead at this stage. But, as always, she seemed to possess an innate ability to throw a spanner in the works, and ruin his plans. *Not this time,* he thought.

KRUGER SAT in the operations room, his feet up on the edge of the holo-table. He was cleaning his nails with a long knife. It had a serrated blade and looked like a tool more suited to gutting sharks than to giving a manicure. Across from him sat Xenon. He was still and silent and exuded a Zen-like calm. VanHoff caught his eye momentarily as he entered the room. He found it hard to break away from his gaze, he felt sucked in, like his soul was laid bare for Xenon to see. He had to drag his eyes away by sheer force of will.

"Ahh... Peter. Excellent timing. I was just discussing with our colonist friend here the need for cooperation and harmony in the colony as we progress to COM governance."

"And how's that going?" said VanHoff as he sat down at the table.

"Very well. We have agreed on a plan to release a small contingent of colonists so that important maintenance tasks can be performed. Assuming full cooperation, and a positive mental attitude, then we can proceed over time to release all colonists into productive duties. Isn't that so?" He directed his question at Xenon.

He simply nodded in reply.

"And what about Malbec?" VanHoff rubbed his temples again.

"I'm glad you asked that." The commander sheathed the knife into a leather scabbard strapped to his belt, with a quick reflex action.

"No sign of her in Colony Two, which leads me to believe that someone is leading us on a merry dance." He fixed his gaze on the Hybrid.

Xenon remained totally unfazed, it seemed to VanHoff that there was very little that could crack his aura of serenity. He almost envied him.

"So," the commander slapped the table. "Tell me, where is she?"

"In Colony Two." Xenon's voice was smooth and calm, so much so that VanHoff had no trouble believing him.

"Bollocks." Kruger leaned across the table. The tenor and amplitude of his reply startled VanHoff, and broke the spell that the Hybrid had conjured.

The commander stood up straight. "If she was there, we would have found her by now. So she isn't, is she?"

Xenon remained silent.

"Okay, let's see if we can realign your memory." He tapped his earpiece and spoke. "Ready? Excellent. It's show time." He turned around to the main monitor. "You may want to have a look at this, Xenon."

An aerial view of the biodome central dais

materialized on screen. Two mercenaries pointed weapons at a group of colonists, who were all on their knees, hands on heads.

He turned back to Xenon. "Now, here's what's going to happen. I'm going to ask you again, and if I don't like what I hear..." his arm moved to point back at the monitor. "One of your friends is going to fry. Got that"

Xenon remained silent.

"So, where is she?"

VanHoff liked this man. Brutal but efficient, a kindred spirit. As for Xenon, VanHoff perceived a note of tension ripple across his calm serene shell. Like a pebble being dropped into a still pool. The commander was not bluffing, everyone knew that.

"I don't hear anything." Kruger cocked a hand behind his ear as if to catch the sound of some distant echo.

"Fine," he said at last. "If that's the way you want to play it, so be it." He turned back to the monitor and tapped his earpiece. "Pick one, and waste them."

On screen a mercenary moved forward and aimed his weapon at the head of a hapless colonist. VanHoff could see the look of sheer terror etch itself on her face. Her body trembled and she mouthed a plea the he couldn't quite make out.

The Commander turned back. "Last chance—no? Okay then."

"No, wait." Xenon finally broke, he lowered his head.

A faint smile cracked across VanHoff's face. *Finally, some results,* he thought.

"I'm listening."

Xenon slowly raised his head and looked at Kruger. His lips parted, ready to utter the truth—then he seemed to hesitate. A strange look came over his face, then VanHoff realized he was not looking at the commander, he was looking past him, at the feed from the biodome. VanHoff followed his gaze.

On screen, one of the mercenaries had doubled over and was on his knees, clawing at his head. His comrade looked unsure of what to do. He was keeping his weapon trained on the colonists, at the same time as shouting down to the distressed mercenary. In the operations room Kruger finally realized that both Xenon and VanHoff had their eyes fixed on the screen, he turned around to see what was happening.

"What the..." He tapped his earpiece. "Talk to me."

Currently none of the weapons in the biodome were set to stun. A thought that ran through the Commander's mind as he watched the demented mercenary raise his PEP and fire it at his comrade. Fortunately, he missed.

"Shit... take him out—now!" the commander screamed into his earpiece. But the mercenary bolted off into the undergrowth of the biodome before his comrade had a chance to return fire."

"Benson, go after him... find him, and take him down!"

The colonists were beginning to panic and, seeing their chance, they ran for the now open tunnel exit. VanHoff watched all this with a sense of rising trepidation. A phrase that one of his old board members kept using, back when they first discovered that Colony One was still functioning, came into his head. *What if it's happening again?* But before he could finish this particular line of thought a scream echoed around the main colony facility. It sounded to VanHoff like it came from the medlab. The commander was already on the move, barking orders to the COM mercenaries in the operations room with them. "You, stay here and keep an eye on the hybrid. And you, Slade, come with me." VanHoff followed after them, racing through the facility to the medlab. They stopped and took up positions either side of the medlab door. The commander shouted in. "Dr. Molotov!" No answer. He signaled for Slade to enter, then followed in behind him.

The doctor was lying on the floor, blood oozing from a head wound. Standing over him, holding a long steel bar, was the taikonaut they had brought in earlier. The commander raised his weapon to shoot.

"Don't kill him," VanHoff shouted.

"What? He's a homicidal maniac."

"No, don't kill him, I need him."

The commander gave VanHoff a wary look, then tilted his weapon to set it on stun, and fired. The taikonaut did a kind of chicken dance for a second as his nerve endings spasmed from the electrical overload. Then he dropped on top of the doctor.

"I hope to hell you know what you're doing. Next time I take him out—permanently." The commander nodded to Slade. "You go and help Benson in the biodome. I'll deal with this."

KRUGER LIFTED up the unconscious taikonaut and strapped him down to one of the operating tables. VanHoff checked on the status of the clone Nills. All good, vitals looked stable. Only then did he turn his attention to the doctor. He was still alive, the wound on his head looked worse than it actually was. He sat him up and after a minute he began to come around.

"What the hell happened?" Kruger leaned over him like a storm cloud about to burst.

The doctor lifted a feeble hand as if to wave off the impending threat. "He just suddenly woke up. Started saying something about his head, something like *he couldn't get them out*. I went over to talk to him and he just whacked me on the skull."

"What do you mean, *he couldn't get them out*?"

The doctor said nothing, just shrugged his shoulders.

"Well it all sounds pretty goddamn weird to me." Kruger stood upright and took a few steps back from the doctor.

VanHoff turned around to him. "I think it's all under control now, Commander. I can take it from here."

The commander leaned in, his face close to VanHoff. "In case you haven't noticed, there is a crazy on the loose in the biodome and a population of panicked colonists trying to get out. So I would say things are far from being under control."

VanHoff raised himself up as best he could and answered the commander's stare. "You are here to do a job, now I suggest you go do it."

There was a momentary silence, as taut as a fully wound spring. Kruger backed off, unclipped a small PEP weapon from his waistband and set it down on the workbench. "Part of my job is to keep people alive. So use this if you have to."

VanHoff nodded reluctantly.

"I've set it to stun. Don't want you killing any of us by mistake." He spun around and headed out of the medlab.

IF THERE WAS one thing that Kruger enjoyed more than having everything under control, it was when everything was totally out of control. He was in his element in these situations, it was an addictive adrenaline rush that made life worth living. When things were just on the edge, ready to spiral into chaos, that's when Willem Kruger felt most alive. Now, as he raced across the common room to the biodome door, he felt a wave of excitement ripple through him as he reviewed the current situation.

There was no doubt in his mind that his crew were exposed to the same infection that he had feared might happen. The COM mission hierarchy had gone to great pains to dismiss this scenario as highly unlikely, but

Kruger was not paid to live in the *unlikely*. His worth lay in situations where the shit had hit the fan.

So far one of the Xaing Zu crew had gone over to the dark side. He should have killed him when he had the chance. But at least he was incapacitated, and now out of the fight. The colonists had also seen fit to corral the rest of the Chinese in one of the food processing pods, so they too were rendered inactive. His thoughts now turned to his own COM crew. Already one had gone feral in the biodome. But his major concern was how many more would succumb to this psychotic malaise. A horrific thought struck him—*could he too become infected?* And how would he even know? He put these thoughts out of his mind and concentrated on the current active threats, and how best to contain them. He checked his weapon.

As Kruger approached the tunnel entrance to the biodome he could hear screaming and yelling emanating from within. He pressed his hand to his earpiece. "Slade, Benson, talk to me. I'm approaching the entrance to the biodome, what's the situation?"

Stay frosty, he's heading your way, commander.

With that a number of colonists ran out through the tunnel, they didn't even skip a beat when they saw him. This was not a good sign, as the threat that he posed to them obviously paled in comparison to what they were running from.

A blast from a PEP weapon split the air ahead of him and a colonist collapsed in a writhing heap of flashing light. It snaked and swirled around his body before finally extinguishing itself. The colonist's forward momentum kept him sliding along the floor right up to Kruger's feet. He resisted the temptation to look down and check on the immobilized colonist, his ingrained training instead keeping him focused on the threat, fortunately for Kruger, as the crazed mercenary now came into view.

He was moving at speed towards the commander, but his gait was awkward and he seemed to be rolling his head as he ran. Kruger raised his weapon to take a shot, but he was too slow, a bolt of incandescent light burst out from the mercenary's weapon. Kruger threw himself sideways as the flash passed him by. He hit the floor, rolled and came around for a shot, but something was wrong. His left side was not responding. His arm was paralyzed, he must have been hit. All he could do was watch as the crazed mercenary sped past him, knocking over panicked colonists like ninepins as he barreled forward.

"Guys, talk to me, I'm down, he's getting past me. Where the hell are you?"

"Here, Commander." Kruger looked up and saw lieutenants Benson and Slade standing over him. Benson offered him a hand up. "You okay, sir?"

"Bastard winged me. My left arm is non-operational for a while." He stood up and gripped the weapon tight in his good arm and looked down through the biodome entrance tunnel. The flow of panicking colonists had stopped. Those still inside, which was the bulk of them, had chosen to stay there, assuming it to be the safer option, which from where Kruger was standing made perfect sense.

"Listen to me, Benson. I want you to get VanHoff and the doctor out of the medlab, get them into EVA suits and bring them to the safe zone we identified. You know where that is?"

"Yes sir. What about the biodome door, and the escaped colonists?"

"Screw them. They're too scared to do anything but hide. The ones still in the biodome aren't going anywhere. We can round up the stragglers later. First *you* need to get VanHoff to the safe zone. We will track down this crazy bastard. Got it?"

"Got it, sir." Lieutenant Benson ran off to the medlab.

Kruger watched him go as he took a moment to rub some feeling back in to his arm, then he took a look around. The colonists that had escaped from the biodome were nowhere to be seen, save for the one lying on the ground in front of him. He wondered if he was dead and then he saw the gentle rise and fall of his chest. *He's okay, he'll live—probably.* Kruger checked his weapon again, gripped it tight, and moved off in the direction of the operations room. This was also the access route to the other sectors of the facility. The situation was still volatile, but he was back in the saddle and on the hunt for live game. God, he loved this job.

IT TOOK VanHoff a few moments to regain his composure after facing off with the commander. He ignored the weapon Kruger had left on the workbench and instead focused his attentions on Dr. Molotov, who was now strapping his head with a bandage and checking himself in the mirror. "Going to need a few stitches I should think," he said as he gingerly touched the wound above his temple. VanHoff, seeing Molotov was okay, turned back to look over the unconscious Xaing Zu taikonaut. Now that the mayhem had been brought under control, a slow realization had been building in his mind since observing the incident in the biodome. This realization was now becoming fully formed as he stared down at the face of this crazed individual. "Could it be happening again?" he said to no one in particular.

"What was that you said?" Dr. Molotov was applying an adhesive bandage to close his wound.

"There's only one thing that could make this guy and the COM mercenary in the biodome go crazy like that."

Dr. Molotov spun around and stared at VanHoff for a moment. "You mean there's another one?"

"Yes. In the biodome. A while ago, one of our own crew went crazy, started shooting up the place."

The doctor walked over and looked down at the taikonaut. "We'd better get an IV into him, keep him sedated. We don't want him going nuts again." He pulled out a cannula from a drawer beside the operating table and cracked open the seal.

While Dr. Molotov set about ensuring the

unfortunate Chinese crewmember was well out of harm's way, VanHoff's mind began to race with the implications of these chaotic events. If his suspicions were true then there was only one sure way to find out. So, it was with shaking fingers that VanHoff drew a vial of blood from the patient's arm. If it was truly happening again then he wouldn't need much blood to confirm it.

He prepared a slide and slid it under the microscope. He leaned in to look through the eyepiece, and slowly nudged the focus. His point of view moved around the sample, nothing looked out of the ordinary. But then he stopped and froze. There it was, a clump of dark elongated bacteria. There was no mistaking it. His heart skipped a beat and he snapped his head away from the microscope eyepiece.

"What is it?" Dr. Molotov looked over at him.

VanHoff waved a hand to silence him. This was a seminal moment. The thing that he had been searching for, the thing that had been denied him so many times—here it was at last. He peered in through the microscope eyepiece again. He was afraid that he might have been imagining it, that it wasn't really there. He scanned the sample for a few more moments before saying, "I've found it."

Then a thought came to him like a hammer blow, the genetic miracle that he had been searching for his whole life was probably already inside him, infecting him, changing his biology. He wondered if that was the reason for the headache that had been rumbling around the folds of his brain since morning. Yet, he had not gone mad like the others. He felt the skin on the back of his hand as if to find some physical evidence that the bacteria was working its magic on him. But this was ludicrous, his excitement was dulling his scientific mind, there was a better way to be certain. A few moments later, Peter VanHoff again peered into the microscope at the dark elongated shapes of the Janus bacteria. Except this time he was looking at a sample of his own blood. He sat back. A broad smile broke across his aged face. He had done it. He had found it at last.

But he didn't get time to revel in his triumph, as a wave of screaming and yelling emanated from somewhere outside the medlab. He stopped and listened as the mayhem slowly died down. He was just about to relax again when Lieutenant Benson burst through the door.

"Dr. VanHoff, Dr. Molotov. You'd better come with me. Right now!"

18

CHAOS

So far her plan was having the desired effect, causing chaos and mayhem to run riot in the colony. COM was off balance, losing control of the colonists now running out of the biodome in panic. The medlab had also been evacuated. The battle had begun, but Jann had to act now if the momentum were to stay in her favor. She turned around to Gizmo. "Time to go, come on."

They raced over to the airlock door that gave them access through the short tunnel to the medlab. Within minutes they had ascended to the ancillary medlab module. Jann peered through the small window in the door and scanned the room. It was empty save for Nills lying on one of the operating tables and one of the Chinese crew strapped down to another.

"Okay," she whispered to Gizmo. "Once we're inside you need to get that main door closed."

"Will do."

She cracked open the door and stepped inside. Gizmo whizzed, as silently as possible for a robot on tracks, over to the entrance door and closed it gently. Jann moved to where Nills lay. His face was pale, and from his body ran a profusion of wires and tubes. But his vitals looked good as they drew themselves out on the monitors. Her first reaction was to start pulling out the invasive tubes but that might not be such a bright idea. She needed to calm herself down and figure out what each one was doing. Only then could she start to bring him back to the real world.

Outside she could hear the colony descending into chaos. Yelling and screeching interspersed with the telltale whoomp of a PEP weapon being discharged. Gizmo had explained the operation of these weapons to her, so she dearly hoped that they had set them to stun. The last thing she wanted was the death of a colonist because of her high-stakes gamble. An alarm shrieked on the monitor as she withdrew a tube from Nills' upper arm. She jumped, then tapped the screen to switch it off. The noise from outside was getting louder. After a few more anxious minutes she finally extracted the last of the IVs, the one that kept him sedated. She pulled it gently from his neck and held her finger over the insertion point to stem the blood. She looked up at the monitor, all was okay, his vital signs were holding steady.

The medlab door burst open and in rushed two

colonists, dragging a third along the floor between them. They stopped in surprise when they saw her and Gizmo.

"Dr. Malbec... we thought you were dead... how did you survive the tunnel collapse?"

Jann looked down at the body of the colonist that they had deposited on the floor. "Is he dead?"

"Eh... I don't think so... I'm not sure."

"Gizmo, go check on him." Jann was in the process of applying bandages to the numerous punctures on Nills' body.

"Low but steady pulse, some pupil dilation, some scorching of the cervical epidermis." The droid looked up at Jann. "Not dead. Injuries symptomatic of plasma energy pulse weapon set on *paralyze*."

This was good news to Jann. At least the COM mercenaries had seen fit to show some restraint, having presumably established that killing them all would not be in their best interests. After all they were not the enemy—yet. They were simply running in panic from the infected. That said, non-lethal weaponry had the advantage of enabling the user to disable anyone with impunity. So they could, if they wanted to, turn the tables very quickly. Jann knew she didn't have much time. If she hoped to regain control she would have to act fast. She eyed the PEP weapon that VanHoff had forgotten to take with him when he was unceremoniously whisked out of the medlab. She had spotted it earlier, but now Jann reached over and picked it up. It was small and stubby, but surprisingly heavy.

"What's going on out there?" she said to the others.

They all stopped and listened. It had gone very quiet. No one spoke for a moment. Jann inched her way to the main door and opened it a crack. What she could see of the outside area seemed empty of people. She turned back to the colonists. "How many people got out of the biodome?"

"I don't know... the door was open so we just ran. One of the COM mercenaries went totally crazy in there... shooting up the place."

"Gizmo, can you get any location data on the COM mercenaries?"

"I'm picking up readings from multiple sectors."

"Your best guess for where they are now?"

"There is a cohort heading for dome five. Their signature shows patterns symptomatic of multiple high energy sources."

"PEP weapons?"

"Precisely."

"And the operations room?"

"I estimate one, maybe two lifeforms."

"Okay, well it looks as if Xenon is still in there, so here's the plan. You guys stay here and keep an eye on Nills and your colleague. Myself and Gizmo will go and find Xenon."

"What about him?" The colonist pointed over to the unconscious taikonaut.

"He isn't going anywhere."

The colonist wasn't convinced. "Are you sure?"

"Trust me. He's strapped down good and tight." She moved back to the door, opened it a bit wider and scanned the area. It was deserted.

"Okay Gizmo, let's go."

PETER VANHOFF FOLLOWED close behind Lieutenant Benson as they navigated their way to the safe zone. Dr. Molotov took up the rear. This was an area within the facility that the commander had deemed the safest place to hole up should the situation become volatile. As a precaution, EVA suits had been stashed there along with other necessary supplies.

VanHoff had followed along in a kind of daze, not really paying attention to where they were going. His mind was still trying to fathom the enormity of his discovery. Not how it came to be that the Janus bacteria had suddenly materialized after so much time lying dormant, but more about how it was multiplying in his bloodstream and what that meant for his own flawed biology. He had sought this moment for so very long that now it had arrived, he felt like he was in a dream.

"You need to get into this EVA suit, sir."

"What?" He was snapped back to the here and now by the mention of the words, *EVA suit.*

"The suit, sir. You need to put it on." Benson motioned at it with a nod of his head.

Under normal circumstances VanHoff would have

balked at the thought of encasing himself in an EVA suit unless it was absolutely necessary, such was his fear of being enclosed in one. He had barely kept it together for the few short steps it took to get from the rover to the entrance airlock when they arrived. But now his fear was virtually nonexistent, it had evaporated. The claustrophobic environment held no threat for him. With the bacteria now working its miracle within, he felt invulnerable, invincible, even superhuman. Yet, he knew all this was purely psychological, any improvement in his physiology would take time to be evidenced. Nevertheless, it was a fundamentally different VanHoff that now inspected the EVA suit, than the VanHoff that landed on Mars, not so long ago.

"It's just a precaution, sir. In case we need to get you out of here in a hurry."

Dr. Molotov was already suiting himself up, so VanHoff nodded. "Sure, no problem, I understand." He moved over to where the EVA suit was hanging and started to get it ready to put on. He was opening up the front and just in the process of performing the initial checks on the suit system when he noticed that Benson had a vacant, distracted look. "Are you okay?"

Benson looked back at him with a kind of confused expression. Like he couldn't quite remember where he was. VanHoff felt an anxious twinge ripple through him as he considered that Benson might be succumbing to the infection, and not in a good way.

Benson seemed to snap out of it. "Sorry, sir. Just kind

of... zoned out for a moment." He shook his head and touched his earpiece, listening to some message from the commander, no doubt. "Gotta go. Will you be okay here, sir?"

"Yeah, we'll be fine. Go. You need to get this facility back under control."

Benson nodded and headed off. VanHoff watched him go. He wondered if he should inform Kruger of his suspicions about the mental health of the mercenary. Maybe not, perhaps he was just being a bit paranoid. Best leave the commander do his job.

As Jann and Gizmo entered the common room, they startled a group of colonists that had hidden out in there. They were armed with hastily constructed weapons such as spears, clubs, and knives from the galley that were now repurposed and brought into emergency service.

"It's me... it's me." She held her hands up and moved into the light so they could see her better. One by one they moved out from alcoves and the dark corners of the space. "Dr. Malbec, you're alive!"

"Yes, it's me, still here. Where are the others?"

They looked from one to the other. "Scattered... I think. One of the mercenaries went nuclear in the biodome, everyone ran."

"It's that crazy bug, isn't it? It's starting to happen again... oh god we're all going to go insane."

"No, you're not. And yes, it is that *crazy bug*, but colonists are immune to it, we all are. So it's just COM and the Chinese that have to worry." Jann's words had a visible calming effect on the ragtag group. It was only then that she noticed the colonists had kept quite a distance from each other, fearing that at any moment a friend might flip and drive a stake though their heart.

"How can you be so sure that's what it is? I thought it had died out, long ago."

"No. A small sample remained. I released it into the colony environment last night."

"Holy crap, so it's true?

Jann smiled. "Yes, and we now have them on the run. So we need to pull together and take back control."

"What should we do?"

"Xenon is being held in the operations room, we need to get him out. But we need to be careful, there may be a COM mercenary in there with him."

The colonists all gripped their makeshift weapons tighter and moved closer to Jann and Gizmo. They were ready for the fight.

The operations room was the nerve center for Colony One. All systems could be monitored and managed from there. It had one main door, with a long window along the wall facing out onto the concourse that connected several different sectors of the facility. One side led to domes four, five and accommodation. Another side had a short connecting tunnel which led to the common room and farther on to the biodome, medlab and a raft of other sectors. They were all now moving through this connecting tunnel but stopped once they reached the concourse intersection. Jann looked across at the operations room window. It was blacked out, no way to see in.

"Gizmo, any movement around here?"

"Data indicates lifeforms located in various sectors, none in close proximity, save for two in the operations room. But this is only an estimate based on ambient temperature readings and sundry data."

Jann hefted the PEP weapon, looking it over to get a feel for how it worked. Maybe it had an *on* switch. She didn't want to be in a situation, needing to pull the trigger, only for nothing to happen. A small screen on the side displayed *ready*. She took this to be a good sign. Below it were a series of bars, which she reckoned must be charge or perhaps shots. It displayed 9. Other than that she couldn't figure much more about it. Whether it was set to stun or lethal she couldn't tell. Maybe it didn't have such a setting. The only real way she could test it would be when she fired off a shot. But if she were to enter a fight she needed to trust her weapon and this was not good enough. She thought about giving it to Gizmo, and instead using a spear one of the colonists was carrying. But it looked too bent and twisted, no good for straight flight. There was nothing else to do, she would have to chance it.

Jann nodded to the others and they followed her quietly across the concourse, lining themselves up on either side of the operations room door. Surprise was the only way this was going to work. But the mercenary inside might already be on high alert, with an itchy trigger finger, waiting for some crazed comrade to come bursting through the door and attack. But then she thought, *that might help us.* She whispered her instruction to the others, then counted silently down from three—and kicked the door in.

She dropped down to the floor as a blast of plasma energy screamed over her head out though the open door and dissipated in a crackling wave across the far wall of the concourse. She knew her direction now, rolled over, sighted her target, and fired.

A ball of flashing brilliance enveloped the mercenary. It burst out across his body encasing it in a fiery mesh of flashing light. He shook and jerked as his coordination broke down under the massive surge in electrical signals now overloading his nervous system. Sparks exploded from various electronic equipment he had strapped to his person. No longer able to stand upright he collapsed across a control desk. It too began to pop and spark, as monitors flickered on and off. Finally he slumped to the floor as the last of the plasma burst fizzled out. His eyes were wide, his body still and a thin filament of smoke rose from his skull.

"Holy crap."

"Go check on him." Jann waved to one of the colonists now coming through the door. She ran over to where Xenon was crouched down. One arm covered his head, the other was zip tied to the bar that ran around the edge of the comms desk. He poked his head out and looked up.

"Jann. I thought you were dead." A look of surprise burst on his face.

"Yeah, I'm still alive. It's hard to get rid of me. Gizmo, can you get these zip ties off?"

The little droid selected a suitable tool from its inventory and snapped off the nylon cuffs. Xenon stood up. "How did you survive the tunnel collapse?" He was rubbing his wrist.

"That doesn't matter. What matters is getting control back. We have an opportunity now, so we need to grab it."

"What's going on? Everyone is running around, going crazy."

"You remember the Janus bacteria?"

"Yes. It decimated the original colony. But that was destroyed a long time ago."

"Not exactly. There was one sample remaining—and I released in to the colony environment last night."

Xenon eyes went wide. "I see. Well that would explain a lot."

"But don't worry, all colonists are immune to it. It will only affect COM... and the Chinese."

"Very clever. So they're all going insane."

"Not all, just some. But enough to throw a very crazy cat or two among some very scared pigeons."

Xenon smiled. "So we have a chance to get rid of them?"

"No." Jann grabbed his arm and looked hard at him. "We cannot let them leave the planet. That would be a disaster. We can't let them bring this back to Earth."

"Ah... I see. No, that would not be good."

Gizmo's head twitched.

"What is it?"

"Movement... multiple sectors."

"Can we see from here?"

Gizmo tapped at the control desk. "The network is down. The electrified COM mercenary shorted out a lot of circuits. It will take time to get them repaired." A few sparks exploded from the desk as Gizmo tested it. "This could take a while."

Dr. Peter VanHoff had finally encased himself in his EVA suit, but left the helmet off for the moment. It would only take a few seconds to attach it, should the need arise. And he was hoping that was not going to happen. He had briefly contacted Kruger on his comms but got no information from him other than, *sit tight and wait until you get the all clear.* So he and Dr. Molotov sat on an old storage container. VanHoff occupied himself with his thoughts as he waited.

The reason he had come to Mars in the first place was to find the very thing that was now inside him, working to restore his flawed genetics. He had so far escaped the negative side effect, insanity. So he felt a deep calm wash over him, something that he had not felt for as long as he could remember. It bathed him in a warm glow of peace and contentment, mixed with a dash of anticipation—the future looked good, very good for Peter VanHoff.

It struck him then that he did not need to be here anymore. Not in this safe zone, not in Colony One, not even on this planet. Now that he had found it, what need was there for him to remain? He could return to Earth. Sure, there were a few practical issues to deal with. But to all intents and purposes it was *job done*, time to go home.

Yet there was always a possibility that the Janus bacteria would not work to counter the effects of his genetic disease, as it did with those who were not so afflicted. So more scientific investigation might be needed to divine its function. But this could be better realized in a fully resourced genetics lab back on Earth, than in the rudimentary facilities here on Mars.

He thought about contacting Kruger again but decided it might be best not to bother him. He was probably busy trying to contain the various members of the crew that had gone psychotic. Assuming, of course, that the commander himself had not succumbed. And if he had, then how would VanHoff get out? He looked around the space that they had been sequestered in. It was subterranean, that much he knew. But was there a way out from here on to the Martian surface? And even if he could find a way there was still the long walk back to the COM ship. Could he handle that? He was more confident now in undertaking such an arduous journey.

Physically he should be able to manage it. It would be controlling his debilitating claustrophobia that would be the challenge. However, he felt sure he could overcome it. With the flight officer ready and waiting, and everything prepped, he could, in theory, leave the planet and return to Earth.

The only problem with this plan was he could not see a way out of here, save for going back into the facility and exiting via one of the usable airlocks. It was doable. But it would mean exposing himself to more danger than was necessary. So he decided to wait. Well, he would give it another thirty minutes. Then, if there was no resolution, he and Dr. Molotov would attempt to leave this place and make their way back to the MAV, and ultimately off this hellhole of a planet.

19

JING TZU

I t had gotten quiet, too quiet. Jing Tzu stood with his ear pressed against the locked door of the food processing pod, where he and the two other Xaing Zu crew had been imprisoned. Outside in the biodome nothing could be heard. Something was going on, and he didn't like it.

A short while after Xenon and the other colonists had unceremoniously dumped them in here, the biodome descended into chaos. Shouting, yelling, the sound of a PEP weapon, then running. Now there was a deathly silence. Yet it could be an opportunity.

He and his crew needed to get out of here somehow. Better still, would be to get off the planet and return to Earth. They would have to leave sometime, COM couldn't hold them here forever. But he didn't trust them either. He wouldn't put it past that maniacal VanHoff to just blow them out of an airlock.

He pressed his ear against the door again—silence.

"Anything?" His first officer, Chen Deng, called over from the back of the pod. He had finished tying up their mission geneticist, who had started to get that same strange look in his eyes that Dan Ma had just before he went psychotic. So they decided to tie him up, much to his consternation, before he started killing them all. He protested for quite a while before finally zoning out, or maybe he was unconscious, Chen couldn't tell. Commander Jing Tzu moved away from the door and shook his head. "Nothing." He looked down at the geneticist. "How is he?"

"Well, if he wakes up and goes ballistic, like Dan Ma, at least we've got him contained."

"We need to get out of here, back to the lander if possible. There's something going on out there, and I have a bad feeling about it. However, it might just give us an opportunity."

"Back to the lander? How? We'd need our EVA suits."

"Well you can stay here and go insane if you want."

Chen looked down at the unconscious geneticist. "What's happening to them?"

"It's this place, it's possessed by a corrupt biology. One that eats away at the mind. They warned us about it, remember?"

"But it was supposed to be eradicated."

"Well, you can stay here and think about it if you like, or you can help get us out of this place."

Chen stood up. "So we just leave him here... and Dan Ma as well?"

"Screw him. He's a geneticist, the very people who create these abominations." Jing Tzu moved closer to Chen and calmed his voice. "Two of our crew are dead, killed by COM. Dan Ma is probably dead too or may as well be." He looked down at the geneticist. "And we can guess what's going to happen to him. So the mission is over. There is nothing to be gained by staying here. We need to grab this chance and try to escape."

Chen looked at him for a moment and eventually nodded. "You're right, let's get the hell out of here."

It took them less than five minutes to break open the pod door. They stepped out into the biodome and looked around. It was still and silent. "Where are they all?" Chen whispered.

Jing Tzu didn't answer, instead he was looking high up to the biodome roof trying to spot cameras. "Come." He moved into where the undergrowth would hide them from any prying eyes. Chen followed. When Jing Tzu was sure they were well hidden he broke a small twig from a bush, hunkered down and started drawing in the dirt.

"We're here. Over here is the airlock with our spare EVA suits. The only problem is that was damaged by COM in the attack. So the suits may also be damaged."

"They might not even be there," said Chen.

"True. Also, there is a distinct possibility that the

colony is in lockdown. If that's the case then none of the airlocks will be operational."

"Great."

"However, there is another option." He started scratching again with the twig. "This is the operations room, over here. Beside it is the storage pod where we put some of the additional equipment we brought. There should be some more spare EVA suits in there somewhere."

"That sounds like a better plan to me. But, assuming we find the suits, how do we get out?"

"There is an access route, around here, that goes down into the soil processing area."

"But that's subterranean, how's that going to help us?"

"There is an automatic airlock system for the soil harvesting robots." He looked up at Chen. "It doesn't go into lockdown."

Chen looked at the commander's scratchings for a moment. "Okay, let's do it."

THEY MOVED THROUGH THE BIODOME, sticking to the areas where the vegetation was thickest, hoping it would keep them concealed from view. They passed along the dense rows of hydroponics and finally to where the main entrance door stood, wide open. "Come on, let's keep going." They hurried to the side of the door, keeping low and quiet. Jing Tzu looked down the length of the short tunnel. "Clear, let's go."

They hugged the tunnel wall as they moved along and out into the main common room. "This way," Jing Tzu signaled and they moved off in the direction of the operations room. They had only taken a few steps when they heard the telltale *whoomp* of a PEP weapon, followed by a scream, followed by footsteps—running their way.

Jing Tzu dived out of sight behind a low counter, Chen followed behind. They waited as the footsteps grew louder. It sounded like multiple people, running fast. As they charged past they could see they were colonists, carrying two others, all heading in the direction of the medlab. As soon as they were out of sight Jing Tzu rose from his hiding place and nodded to Chen to follow him. They moved with caution, keeping their ears alert to any danger.

When they arrived at the concourse it was deserted, but they could see shadows moving behind the smoked glass window of the operations room. Somewhere far off in the depths of the facility they could hear shouts.

Jing Tzu put his finger to his lips and pointed in the direction of the storage pod. Chen nodded his understanding and they tiptoed across the concourse, all the time keeping an eye on the movements within the operations room. They reached the door to the storage pod, as the racket emanating from deep within the facility was getting louder and more frenetic.

The door was locked. "Shit. I don't suppose you know the code?" Jing Tzu was pushing his shoulder to it trying to break it open.

"Here, let me try." Chen pushed Jing Tzu out of the way and tapped at the keypad a few times. The door clicked open. He looked over at Jing Tzu and winked. "It's good to pay attention to the details sometimes." They bundled themselves inside.

Automatic lights flickered on, illuminating a chaotic scene of equipment and storage strewn all around the space. They stood with their backs to the door looking out across the tumbled landscape.

"We're never going to find anything in here." Chen scanned the jumble of crates and boxes.

"There should be at least three spare EVA suits in here somewhere, and the sooner we find them the sooner we can get off this rock." Jing Tzu started sorting through the detritus, reading labels, righting boxes.

"Commander Jing." Chen was on the other side of a mound of equipment.

"Did you find them?"

"No, but I found something else."

Jing Tzu moved over to look at where Chen was pointing. Sitting on the floor, partially covered by a tarpaulin was Yutu. He looked over at his First Officer and smiled. "This is good fortune indeed. Maybe even auspicious." He reached down and ripped the cover off. The robot looked undamaged, but inactive, no power lights. Jing Tzu slid open a metal panel on the robot's back, revealing a small flat screen, with several switches arrayed on either side. He flicked a number of them and the screen lit up, then placed his palm momentarily on the screen so it could be scanned. The robot twitched and the screen filled with scrolling code as the boot-up sequence began to reanimate the machine.

The robot rose up from its haunches and moved several of its limbs as if testing their function. Jing Tzu and Chen stood back as it performed its systems checks. When it finished it raised its head and spoke. "Commander Jing Tzu, First Officer Chen Deng. I am at your service."

"Debrief, show last visual." Jing Tzu instructed.

Yutu's eyes flickered and a 3D image was projected into the space in front of the robot. It showed the main airlock exploding inward as the COM assault began. COM had set up an outer umbilical so the facility would not lose atmospheric integrity when it blew. Smoke and dust filled the scene, punctuated by streaks of bright blue plasma bursts from the PEP weapons. Then a COM mercenary came into view and aimed something at the robot. The visual ended abruptly.

"Replay—data only," said Jing Tzu.

This time Yutu projected a stream of stylized data for the time period. It was part environmental: what existed in the space around the robot at the time, and part internal: what was happening to its own systems.

"There, stop." Jing Tzu pointed into space. "A massive electromagnetic spike. That's what disabled Yutu."

"I thought it was hardened against EMP from a PEP weapon."

"It is, this is different, maybe a direct hit from something designed to overload electronic circuitry."

"Well, at least it didn't damage it. Yutu is designed to shut down immediately to protect its systems. But, I have a better idea."

"What's that?"

"Something that will give them a shock if they try it again." The commander turned back to Yutu. "Access."

The robot stood up on all four limbs as the panel on its back slid open again. Jing Tzu proceeded to tap commands into the interface.

"What are you doing?"

Jing Tzu didn't answer for a few more minutes until he was finished. "Self-destruct." He winked at Chen. "If Yutu senses another attack like that it will give them all a very big surprise."

Chen looked concerned. "Is that wise?"

Jing Tzu spun around, visibly angry at his subordinate questioning his authority. "This place is an abomination. As soon as we are safely on the planet's surface away from here I will instruct Yutu to return— and self-destruct. It will take this place with it. Destroy it, hopefully for good."

The first officer simply nodded. Jing Tzu turned back to the machine. "Yutu, locate spare EVA suits."

The robot moved off, shifting its head this way and that, scanning the area. Like a metal sniffer dog, it poked and prodded with its sensors. It stopped beside three elongated storage containers with the Xaing Zu

Industries logo on the side. "Located." It pointed with one of its forelimbs.

They cracked them open and spent the next few minutes checking the suits' resources. None were fully charged but they were reasonably well resourced otherwise. With the help of the robot they calculated they had enough to make it to the Xaing Zu ship and still have 32.5% resources in reserve, more than enough. A few more minutes and they were back at the entrance door, suited and booted, carrying their helmets.

Jing Tzu stuck his ear to the inside of the door and listened. He could hear muffled sounds far off in the depths of the colony. Whatever was going on was still in play. He opened the door a crack and peered out. Two colonists passed right by, but didn't see him—a moment earlier and they would have. He watched them move along the concourse and finally out of sight, he thought one of them might be Jann Malbec. When he was sure they were gone, he stepped out and looked around, then he signaled to Chen to follow. They moved out of the storage pod as silently as a bulky EVA suit would allow. Yutu followed, hunkered low to the floor. Fortunately they didn't have far to go, just a few meters to the soil processing access door. Jing Tzu opened it while Chen kept watch. They finally slipped inside, unseen.

THE SPACE WAS NARROW, and short. Only a few feet of floor before they started to descend down a steep ramp into the subterranean cave system beneath Colony One. It was designed as an access route for maintenance crews who needed to service the soil processing machinery and harvester robots. The walls and floor of this cave were not sealed and hence the air within had a high concentration of perchlorates. Not something you want to spend much time breathing, as it could cause thyroid problems. But that was the least of their worries, they weren't planning on staying here too long.

It was dark. The hum of machinery grew more intense as they descended. Yutu went ahead, a beam of light flicked on from its head. It slowed down as it probed the area by bouncing a multitude of frequencies around the volume. It stopped, forcing Jing Tzu and Chen to halt.

"What's it doing?"

"Shhh." Jing Tzu held a finger to his lips.

The robot's head tilted this way and that, and just when the commander considered it had stopped completely, it shot off across the cave with impressive speed. A figure darted out from a hiding place and ran. But it didn't get far. By the time Jing Tzu and Chen had caught up with the robot it had both of its forelimbs resting on the shoulders of its victim, pinning him to the floor. The figure held an arm across his face and shouted. "Get this goddamn thing off me."

Jing Tzu looked down at him. It was Peter VanHoff.

20

<hr>

DOME FIVE

As Gizmo worked to repair the operation room console, Jann had a moment to consider their next move. With the limited data that the droid could provide, she began to get a picture of where people were located. The bulk of the *lifeforms*, as Gizmo put it, were in the biodome. This made sense as Jann considered the colonists were too scared to move from whatever hiding places they had found for themselves in there, and if you were of the mindset to lay low and keep out of trouble, then the biodome was the perfect place for it. She also discovered from Xenon that the remains of the Xaing Zu crew were locked up in one of the food processing pods, so at least she didn't have to consider them as an immediate threat.

Of the colonists that had run out of the biodome, some were in the medlab looking after Nills and the injured. The rest were here in the operations room with her. She looked around. Some were tending to the COM mercenary she had just blasted. Surprisingly, he was still alive, lying on the floor unconscious. How long the effects of a blast from a PEP weapon lasted, she had no idea. So he could potentially wake up at any minute and start causing trouble. Although, he was bound to be in considerable pain from all the burns inflicted on him by the exploding electronics. Nevertheless, it would be a good idea to restrain him now, before he came to.

But her main consideration was COM, and how to immobilize them as a threat. Yet, to do this they needed to know where they all were—and where was VanHoff?

"Gizmo, any joy with that console?"

"That depends on how you define joy. There is the joy of fixing, and then there is the joy of having fixed."

Jann looked over at Xenon and sighed. He was in the process of tying up the mercenary. He just nodded at the quirky robot and smiled as if he had read her mind.

"Gizmo, I just want to know where the bulk of the COM crew are located." Jann tried again.

"Well why did you not say so?" Gizmo spun around to face Jann. "The console is too badly damaged for me to effect repairs in any immediate time frame, and I have no visual or audio feeds. So, from the limited amount of data available to me, and extrapolating two-dimensional direction vectors over time, my best guess is the main COM cohort are somewhere in the connecting tunnel between domes four and five, and accommodation."

"And VanHoff?"

"Much as I hate to admit it, but I do not know with any certainty where he is."

"Well, we know he was in the medlab until a short time ago. I would imagine that COM are keeping him close, keeping him safe," said Xenon. He was now examining the PEP weapon belonging to the fallen mercenary.

"Gizmo, can we lockdown the facility so no one can get out?"

The little robot moved to an undamaged section of the operations room and tapped some icons. "It is already locked down."

"Good," said Jann. "Now we just need to isolate COM. Can we close off that sector?"

"Yes, but unfortunately I can not do this remotely." Gizmo swiveled his head back to look at Jann. "Come, let me show you." It moved over to the holo-table and brought up a 3D schematic of the colony. "This door here will close off the entire sector from the rest of the colony. No way out for COM. But you must do this manually."

Jann considered this for a moment, then stood back from the holo-table and faced the others. "Okay, so here's what we do..." But before she had time to explain her plan a COM mercenary appeared in the doorway to the operations room. He just stood there, not moving, and his eyes possessed a very long distance stare.

"Shit." Jann grabbed her weapon and pointed it at him as the others dove for cover. "Drop the weapon!"

The mercenary looked confused. His head tilted to

the side for a moment then looked down at his weapon. He lifted it up and examined it as if its function and purpose had escaped his memory.

"Just drop it!" Jann moved closer, her weapon held with both hands, arms outstretched. Xenon also raised his weapon and pointed at the confused mercenary.

Something suddenly snapped into place in the mercenary's confused mind and several things happened all at once. He let out a long blood-curdling scream that physically stunned them. At the same time he raised his weapon, having somehow remembered its function, and fired a blast before running off.

Jann took a moment to react, and fired. But the mercenary had gone and her shot dissipated off the far wall of the concourse. She ran out the door, followed by Xenon. Jann looked around but he was nowhere to be seen. "Dammit. Where did he come from?"

"It is unlikely he's the same mercenary that went psycho in the biodome. Which means we have a second one to deal with," said Xenon.

Jann was still looking down the concourse in the direction of dome five. "This could work in our favor. It looks like he's headed for the main COM cohort. So if we can get that door closed then they can fight it out between themselves in there." She lowered her weapon and turned back to Xenon. Some of the other colonists had come out of the operations room holding various rudimentary weapons.

"Anyone hit?"

"Yes, Melva. She's alive, but unconscious."

Jann walked back into the operations room. Melva was lying on the floor, flat on her back. A large burn mark, the size of a dinner plate, bloomed out across her chest.

"You'd better get her to the medlab, and take that COM mercenary as well," Jann instructed.

The colonists started to gather up the fallen.

Gizmo, you stay here and get that console back up and running."

"I shall do my best, Jann."

"Xenon. You and I will go and get the door to that sector sealed. If we can do that, then we have a chance at finishing this. Come on, let's go."

COMMANDER WILLEM KRUGER had tracked the psychotic crewmember that had gone ballistic inside the biodome to a cluster of domes on the far side of the facility. These were connected via a short tunnel to a concourse that acted as a kind of backbone for the Colony One infrastructure. Several sectors were linked to this concourse. The area that he and the rest of his crew were now searching consisted of two small domes, collectively named *accommodation,* and two larger ones, each with the unimaginative titles of dome four and dome five. His crew had already conducted a thorough search of all these sectors except for dome five. All were clear. Kruger checked his PEP weapon for the umpteenth time and then signaled for his crew to gather around.

"Okay, listen up. I want this guy taken down quick. I don't care if he's your best buddy, he's now a homicidal maniac ready to gut you on sight. So take him down at the first opportunity. Got it?"

Both Slade and Jones nodded.

"Second thing, and this is very important so pay attention," Kruger paused for a moment and looked over at the entrance to dome five. "There is a methane processing reactor in there, highly volatile."

"Well that's just great."

"Put a sock in it, Jones. It is what it is, so let's just be careful what we're shooting at. The storage tanks are on the outside of the dome so that's something. But do me a favor and try not to shoot the processing unit."

"Why not, sir?" said Slade

Kruger and Jones each gave an exasperated sigh. "Ka-boom. That's why." The commander did an exploding gesture with his hands to emphasize the point. But as he was about to lead them in, a scream echoed from back along the concourse.

"Shit, what the hell was that?" Jones swiveled in its direction, weapon at the ready.

Kruger snapped his fingers. "You stay here. If anyone shows up at that door not looking real friendly, you take them out, no questions."

"Yes sir."

"Slade, you come with me."

They stepped in through the half open door of dome five. It was a large space that was part manufacturing plant, part storage space and part workshop. Strewn here and there were stacks of crates, machine parts and even the skeleton of an old lander module that someone had stripped of all useful components. Kruger moved silently and gave a hand signal that instructed Slade to move out and start searching. It didn't take them long. The deranged mercenary shot out from behind a mountain of crates and fired off two blasts in quick succession. Kruger and Slade dove for cover. A moment later, the commander stuck his head up from behind a crate and scanned the area. The mercenary was nowhere to be seen. He signaled to Slade again to move out. This time Kruger kept his weapon high and ready to fire at the first opportunity.

The whoop of a PEP weapon being fired, back where Kruger had left Jones, stopped them dead in their tracks. "Sounds like Jones has met someone who wasn't real friendly," Slade whispered.

But before Kruger could answer, the mercenary burst out from cover again. This time he didn't get a chance to discharge his weapon. He was encased in a ball of electrical craziness that hit him from two different directions at the same time. He shook and jerked and bounced around like a pinball before collapsing to the floor, incandescent flashes still arcing around his body.

When the light show had finally stopped Kruger and Slade approached the body with caution. He was dead, no question about that. It was job done as far as the commander was concerned so he shouldered his weapon. "Okay, let's get out of here. It's time to start herding the colonists back into the biodome."

They walked off slowly, there was no rush. The thorn in Kruger's side had finally been taken care of. From here on in it would be just a mop up operation.

A scream reverberated around the dome as another deranged COM crewmember came bursting through the door. It was Benson, his weapon aimed in their direction. Before either Kruger or Slade could unshoulder their weapons he fired. It was at that instant that Willem Kruger, commander of the Colony One Mars mission, realized they were both standing right in front of the methane reactor.

"Oh shit," was all he could manage.

JANN AND XENON slowly inched their way down along the concourse, moving on opposite sides, keeping close to the walls. Up ahead on the left was the entrance tunnel to where they assumed the COM mercenaries were. It was set at right angles to the concourse, so Jann crept along and peered carefully around the corner. She signaled to Xenon who darted across and took up a position beside her.

"All clear, as far as I can tell." She ventured another

look around the corner. "Come on, let's get that door closed."

They entered the tunnel, and could now see the door, about halfway along. This was a large circular bulkhead, hinged on one side and opened back against the tunnel wall on their side. Closing this would isolate everything on the far side and lock the COM mercenaries in. Jann hurried forward, but as she came close to the door she thought she could see a body farther in, on the far side, close to the junction for the domes.

"There's someone on the floor down there."

Xenon looked down the tunnel, moving his head around trying to see. "I can just make out a foot."

Jann looked back at Xenon. "Could it be a colonist?"

Xenon said nothing for a moment as he considered this. Then he stuck his head around the side of the door. "Hard to know from here."

Jann stepped out from the wall and started forward. "I'll take a closer look."

Xenon seemed unsure of this decision but didn't protest as Jann moved quietly down the tunnel. She passed the bulkhead door. The foot turned into a leg which eventually turned into the body of a COM mercenary. Jann checked his nametag, *Jones*. He was still alive but had obviously been hit by a PEP weapon. He lay unconscious with a thin trail of smoke rising up from the blast mark. Jann couldn't tell if he had been one of the infected. *Was he the same one that attacked them in the operations room?* She wasn't sure but he seemed shorter, with different color hair, more blond. She looked back at Xenon. "Come on, give me a hand with him."

Xenon stalled for a moment before stepping over the threshold of the bulkhead door. He ran down to her. "Jann, this is very risky."

"Quick, we'll grab one leg each and drag him back."

He did so reluctantly. "I don't see why you're going out of your way for this guy."

"Call it my maternal instinct."

Xenon smiled and nodded.

Jann suddenly lost her balance as the tunnel physically shook with the force of a massive explosion. She dropped the leg she had been dragging and braced herself against the wall. Xenon was doing the same, and staring into her eyes as if to say. *I told you this was a stupid idea.*

She began to feel the atmosphere being sucked out. Not so much that it would knock her over but enough to know that this was serious, and getting more so. A klaxon blared and red strobe lights kicked on overhead.

"What the hell was that?" Jann was getting herself upright again.

"We'd better get out of here." They ran for the door but it was automatically closing. Having detected the drop in pressure the bulkhead was sealing itself to protect the integrity of the main colony facility. It was sacrificing this sector, and all who were in it.

"Hurry!" Xenon dove through the door to the other side, grabbed the edge with both hands and planted his feet against the wall trying to stop it from closing. Jann squeezed in through the gap and just managed to bring her feet in as the door slammed shut. They sat there for a few moments, gasping and calming themselves down. "That was close." Xenon gave a wry smile.

Jann smiled back and looked at the bulkhead door. "Well, I think that solves our COM infestation problem."

After a few moments the alarms stopped just as Gizmo came racing down the tunnel.

"What the hell just happened back there, Gizmo?"

"An explosion in dome five, most probably the methane processing unit. It has caused a significant loss of integrity in that sector."

"Is the rest of the facility safe?"

"Yes, quite safe, now that this bulkhead door is sealed."

"Okay, but we need to get back to operations and check out all the systems. Let's make sure there are no other disasters waiting to jump up and bite us."

BY THE TIME they returned to the operations room, Jann was beginning to sense that it was all over, they had won. Her crazy scheme had paid off. The COM mercenaries in dome five were most likely all dead, including, she surmised, Peter VanHoff. She collapsed into a chair and let out a long, exhausted sigh.

Gizmo started scanning systems, checking integrity,

adjusting levels, establishing that the colony would survive the amputation of one of its limbs.

"Atmosphere nominal, pressure has stabilized."

"Thank god for that."

"Wait a minute."

"What?"

"Oh, nothing major, Jann. I am picking up some infrared readings from the subterranean soil processing area."

"Meaning?"

"Meaning I think there is somebody down there."

Jann sighed. "Oh it's probably just some colonists hiding out." She stood. "Come on, let's go take a look."

21

———

RUN

Jann held the PEP weapon tight as she and Gizmo traversed the narrow passage down into the soil processing area. She had brought it with her just in case and, as they entered the cave, she held the weapon up in front of her and shouted in, "Hello? Anyone there?"

A vague shuffling sound emanated from the back of the cave. "It's okay, you can come out, it's safe now."

The shuffling stopped. Jann looked back at Gizmo. "Stay close." They moved off into the cave and worked their way around a number of storage crates. She stopped short when she finally realized who it was that had been hiding down here.

Two of the Chinese crew, in full EVA suits were standing there, holding up a bloodied and battered Peter VanHoff. On the ground farther back looked to be the unconscious body of another COM crewmember. Jann recognized him as Dr. Molotov. In front of this unlikely quartet stood Yutu. It was staring directly at her, looking like it was ready to pounce. She instinctively pointed the weapon at it. For a moment no one moved, no one said anything. Jann felt like a schoolteacher that had caught two boys beating up on another in the school locker room.

"I see you guys are getting to know one another."

VanHoff seemed to perk up a bit. He looked at her, and a vague scowl grew across his face.

"It's time to pack it in, show's over. Commander Kruger is dead. Colony One is back in our control now." She waved the weapon to signal them to move out.

"I think not." Jing Tzu let go of VanHoff, who collapsed on the ground. "We're getting off this planet, so I suggest you just let us part company. No need for more violence."

"I'd love to, but you can't leave now. You're infected. If you leave you'll be bringing the Janus bacteria back to Earth."

VanHoff seemed to regain some life. He raised himself up. "Don't listen to her, don't listen to anything that comes out of her mouth. She's the cause of all this chaos."

"It's okay, we can eradicate it, we have a way. It'll take a while, but after that I see no reason why you can't go back then. Come on, let's move." She waved the weapon again.

"Don't listen to..." VanHoff tried to speak again but he was cut off.

"You shut up." Chen Deng punched him in the stomach.

"I'm sorry, but we've had enough of this place."

With that Jing Tzu stepped forward and said something in Mandarin to Yutu. The robot shifted slightly then sprang at Jann. She fired the weapon but she was too slow. The robot rammed her in the chest at full force as her shot hit the ceiling and fizzled out. She tumbled backward with the impact, slammed up against a tall stack of storage containers and collapsed on the ground.

The Chinese crew were now running for the automatic airlocks that the harvesters used, putting their helmets on as they went. VanHoff was tottering behind them. Yutu remained, moving slowly towards the fallen Jann.

"Shit, Gizmo... they're getting away."

Gizmo shifted around, reorienting itself in the space, as if it was unsure of what to do. Jann began to pick herself up from the dusty cave floor when she saw the stack of containers lean in towards her; they were falling. She raised her arms up to protect herself, but they all came crashing down on top of her. Her leg was caught under something, she was trapped. Jann tried to pull it free but it held fast. Yutu circled.

"Gizmo, I'm stuck."

The little robot twitched and shifted, extrapolating the probabilities, calculating the odds, and realizing they were not good. It turned its head to Jann. "I do not like that robot." Then it shot off across the floor at high speed and slammed straight into Yutu. The quadruped reacted instantly and was also propelling itself forward when they connected. The two robots tumbled down along the floor, entangled together. Jann could only look on in horror as both machines pulled bits off each other. And it was happening fast, their reaction speed being so much quicker than a human.

They broke apart as Gizmo was flung across the cave. It skidded along the floor, gouging out a deep rut before it came to a halt. But the same instant it was back up on its tracks heading for Yutu at top speed. They slammed into one another again.

Jann pushed and pulled at the container to get it off her leg with all the strength she could muster. It shifted a little, she pushed harder. Time was running out. VanHoff and the Chinese were already at the airlock, trying to hack it open. She had to stop them.

She looked back to see Gizmo and Yutu circling each other. The little droid had sustained considerable damage. Its left arm hung loose at an odd angle, a number of its sensors and antennae were gone completely. The quadruped on the other hand looked to be virtually undamaged. Jann knew that it was only a matter of time before it destroyed Gizmo completely. She searched around for a bar or something she could use as a lever to try and shift the weight pinning her down.

The robots slammed into one another again with a deafening screech of metal on metal. Again Gizmo was flung into the air and skidded to a halt farther up the cave. Jann arched her head to see. It had righted itself, but one of its tracks was broken. It lay on the cave floor like a flattened snake. Gizmo tried to move forward but it fell over.

"No, Gizmo!" she yelled.

Yutu moved in closer, like a jackal stalking its prey, ready to strike the killing blow. Gizmo managed to get itself upright again, and seemed to have calculated a new method of perambulation based on its remaining articulations. It moved using its one functioning arm like a crutch. Then it simply stopped.

Has it just died? she thought. "Gizmo, Gizmo," she shouted.

Yutu crouched low and crept forward, inch by stealthy inch. It sprang high into the air, aiming to land the final blow on Gizmo.

But the little droid had one last trick up its metallic sleeve. As the quadruped reached the apex of its arc, Gizmo fired its taser. Two metal prongs shot out of the little droid, trailing thin spools of wire and buried themselves deep in Yutu's underbelly. The quadruped sparked and shook as 10,000 volts fried its electronics and traumatized its systems. It landed hard on Gizmo, sending the two tumbling across the floor again. When the dust settled, neither moved.

Jann pushed with all her might. The crate shifted a

fraction, enough for her to get free. She looked over to where Gizmo lay, there was no movement. "Gizmo."

She looked past the robot down to the airlocks at the far end. VanHoff and the Chinese were gone, out on the surface. She would have to get back up top and alert everyone. Maybe they still had time to stop them reaching their landers. She dragged herself up to a standing position and tested her legs. They were battered and bruised, but nothing broken. She tottered over to where Gizmo lay and knelt down beside her friend. "Gizmo... Gizmo?"

The little robot twitched and tried to move, but it couldn't seem to manage it. "Oh Gizmo, you're all banged up."

It slowly raised a battered arm and pointed at Yutu, and the little robot spoke just one word, "Run."

"What?" Jann stood up and looked over at Yutu. Its back panel had retracted and a screen flashed a bright red warning. *Self-destruct sequence initiated... Detonation in T-3 seconds.*

"Oh shit." She ran—not fast enough.

The shockwave rammed into Jann's back, lifting her off her feet and she went sailing through the air for what seemed like an eternity, until she finally slammed into the cave wall. She collapsed on the ground like a wet towel. Her eyes were wide and blood oozed from her ears, pooling out across the dusty cave floor.

22

ASTERX LAND

Nills cocked his head up and scanned the sky northward of his position at the edge of the landing site. The atmosphere was clear and bright, there had been no storms recently to kick up dust and create a haze.

"There." Anika's voice echoed in his helmet. He looked to where she was pointing. A long trail streaked across the firmament, growing longer and longer with each passing second. They all watched it as it came closer and the dark smudge at its tip began to resolve. They could now see the chutes trailing out from the top of the craft, swinging and twisting as they fought back against the downward acceleration. Something then detached itself from the base of the craft and plummeted to the planet's surface far off across the horizon.

"Is that the heat shield falling?" Xenon's question seemed to be for no one in particular.

"Yeah, chutes will go soon," Nills replied as he adjusted the anti-glare setting on his visor. Even before he finished his sentence they could see the craft was now in free fall, having slowed itself down as much as it could using primitive fabric. It dropped down towards them with impressive speed. If Nills could cross his fingers in thick EVA suit gloves, he would have done so. The retro-thrusters should fire soon to bring the craft down for a safe landing. Yet it was still plummeting down to the planet with extreme velocity. Just when he thought something must have gone wrong the engines fired and the craft slowed dramatically.

"They're cutting it a bit tight, that's a lot of G to take."

The others didn't reply. They were too transfixed by the unfolding drama.

The craft spun slightly as it descended. Its landing gear started to extend and finally it touched down gently around two kilometers from where Nills, Anika and Xenon were standing.

"Okay, let's go get them." Anika and Xenon clambered onboard the rover, while Nills walked back to the flying bed.

IT HAD TAKEN Nills and the others quite some time to convince AsterX that it was safe to land on Mars and enter Colony One. They had rendezvoused with the old ISA Odyssey orbiter some weeks earlier. They were already well versed in the chaotic events of the combined

COM and Xaing Zu Industries attempts at takeover. Even though that was some months previous, they were still extremely paranoid about the stories of the Janus bacteria that seemed to curse any mission to Mars. So the general feeling of the AsterX team was to keep well clear, forgo any attempt at landing on the planet and instead focus their energies on the main task of the mission. That being to salvage the stranded ISA Odyssey and bring it back into Earth orbit.

However, the situation in Colony One was borderline critical. The explosion in the soil processing area had severely damaged a lot of equipment, not to mention the loss of all processing facilities in dome five. That meant limited water and oxygen production. Not enough to sustain the entire colony. So the council had all agreed that the only option was to move most of the resources and people back to Colony Two. Colony One would be stripped of anything useful, most sectors shut down completely and only a very basic life support left operational to maintain the medlab and a greatly reduced biodome. Everything else would have to be closed up and brought offline. That was about as much as the systems could maintain. Any existing reserves of oxygen would now be used to purge the remaining environment of the Janus bacteria. It took over a month to make the transition before Colony One was finally purged and made safe again.

All this activity was relayed to AsterX until Lane Zebos was finally convinced to take the risk and land.

After all, Nills had communicated over many months with Zebos; on supplies needed, life on Mars, and a myriad of other topics that had fascinated the AsterX CEO. Nills knew he really wanted to land. All he had to do was convince Zebos it was safe, or at least, safe enough.

Nills hit the ignition and each of the four thrusters on the flying bed belched into life. He increased the flow of fuel and the bed began to rise slowly. He nudged the joystick and it gently moved forward, gaining speed as he passed over the slower rover. Far out into the Jezero crater the AsterX landing craft was already disgorging its occupants. He could see two on the surface and one climbing down the exterior ladder.

It was a much smaller craft than the behemoths of COM and Xaing Zu Industries. Reminiscent of the early landers the original colonists had arrived in, but somewhat bigger. It was utilitarian, nothing fancy. Built to do one job and do it well.

The crew had spotted him and were now looking up at this strange craft, this flying bed. Nills nudged the joystick again and the craft slowed to a hover. He reduced the fuel flow and the bed lowered itself back on the surface in a billowing cloud of dust. He clambered down from the open cockpit and started towards the AsterX craft on foot. One of the crew broke away from the main group and headed out to meet him. Nills waved, he waved back and Nills' comms crackled to life.

Nills Langthorp, I presume.

"Yes." By now the crewmember was only a few paces away, he closed the gap and extended a hand.

"Lane Zebos, it's a pleasure to finally meet you." They shook hands like old friends meeting after many years apart.

"So glad you could come," said Nills.

"That's one hell of an entrance you made." Lane was looking over at the flying contraption.

"Yours was pretty spectacular, too. You had us all worried, waiting for those retro-thrusters to fire."

Lane laughed. "You and me both. I was praying to every god I know. Fortunately one of them was listening." He looked over again at the bed. "You must take me for a spin in that sometime."

"You can have a spin in it now, if you like."

Lane hesitated. Nills continued, "Here's the rover." He pointed to a cloud of dust charging across the crater towards them. "They can take your crew and supplies. We can travel on the bed."

"The bed. Is that what you call it?"

Nills laughed. "Yeah, the flying bed."

It took a while for the AsterX crew to organize themselves. They spent most of the time simply looking around or picking up handfuls of Martian dust and letting it fall through their hands as if this simple act could verify, in some way, the truth of their arrival on the planet. Neither Nills nor Anika hurried them, it was a simple pleasure watching the joy they exuded at being here.

But, eventually the rover was packed with initial supplies and the bed also had some equipment strapped on. Nills and Lane clambered on to the open cockpit while the two other AsterX crew got into the rover.

Nills tapped his comms. "See you at Colony One."

"First one there buys the beers," replied Anika.

Nills kept the machine low, not too low that it kicked up dust, yet low enough to experience the ground moving fast beneath it.

"Wow, this is an incredible machine, the only way to travel. When I get back to Earth I want one of these."

"That would be difficult. It's the one-third gravity that makes it possible. On Earth you would need much bigger thrusters and, as you know, a massive fuel tank."

"Gravity's a bitch."

They laughed.

Nills banked the machine to circle back and increased in altitude. He came swooping over the rover as it trundled across the crater. Then he went higher and pointed. "There it is, Colony One."

"Ahh, the fabled El Dorado of the solar system."

"What was that?"

"It's what some people on Earth call it, El Dorado. The legendary cursed city of gold."

"Yeah, I can see how that story would get around. But it's not cursed anymore, we've made sure of that, so you don't need to worry about it. As for the gold, well, I'm afraid it's well past its former glory. Only around twenty percent of it is online."

"Well it still looks incredible."

"If you think this is cool, wait until you see Colony Two."

"Just so you know, Nills, from my perspective, I have died and gone to heaven."

They laughed again.

By the time Nills had finished his scenic route to Colony One, and finally brought the bed in to land, the rover had caught up and was just reversing to the umbilical airlock. This was kept maintained as it was the most efficient way to get people and goods in and out of the rovers. Once connected the rover's interior was now directly connected to the Colony One environment. Nills and Lane entered via the main airlock. The only sections that remained functioning were the common room, operations, a few accommodation pods and the medlab. The biodome was technically still online but it had been stripped of seventy percent of its biomass and was simply put into maintenance mode. All other sectors were closed up and offline.

But it wasn't just physical resources that they had lost, it was also personnel. After all that had happened they now found themselves bereft of any general medical expertise. The COM doctor, Molotov, had died trying to follow VanHoff out of the airlock in the soil processing area. Their second geneticist in Colony Two evacuated with the others when the COM craft departed for Earth.

That left one of the Chinese scientists, stranded now, but purged of the bacteria, so at least he was sane. But, he lacked general medical experience and was totally at sea in dealing with their situation. What Nills really needed was someone with knowledge to help them understand the condition of the patient and give advice on what to do. Fortunately, AsterX had a medical doctor with them, Dr. Jane Foster. And since the communication time between them and the AsterX crew in orbit, was virtually instant, they were able to establish the best treatment that could be provided, given the available resources. But that was some time ago now.

WHEN THEY HAD FINALLY DIVESTED themselves of their EVA suits, Nills was introduced to Chuck Goldswater and lastly to Dr. Jane Foster.

"I suppose you want me to see the patient straight away?" she said.

"That would be great. Follow me, this way." Nills led her across the common room, through the connecting tunnel and into the medlab. He gestured in the direction of the bed. Lying there was Dr. Jann Malbec, her life charted out in waves and graphs on a myriad of different monitors. All about her body, a profusion of tubes and wires sprouted. Her chest rose and fell in a steady rhythm.

After the explosion in the soil processing cave, they had found her barely alive and with severe brain damage.

With the help of Dr. Foster's advice they put her into a coma, and she had been in it ever since.

The AsterX doctor now checked the stats on the monitors, then started on a series of seemingly simple tests: shining a light to check pupil dilation, running a pen along the sole of the foot. After a while she stepped back and looked at Nills.

"I'll be straight with you. It's unlikely she'll ever come out of it. Her brain is too badly damaged, I'm sorry, but there's nothing anyone can do for her now."

23

WHILE YOU WERE ASLEEP

Sounds and shadows drifted in and out of Jann's subconscious. Tendrils of reality coalescing into fragments of cognition. Bubbles of coherence percolated in her brain as it tried to reassemble its shattered matrix. At first these inputs were lost along damaged pathways, fizzling out at dead-ends, extinguished by misfiring synapses. But as time progressed fragmented connections reestablished themselves, laid down new conduit and reformed their structures. Yet, in the confused carnage that was Jann Malbec's brain tissue, alternative undamaged areas had stepped up to the plate to provide interpretation and analysis of exterior stimuli.

Even with all this cellular and synaptic reconstruction going on inside her cranium it took a long time before she had what most people would consider a thought. It came after her receptor infrastructure gained sufficient bandwidth to process incoming data and assign it labels: sound, light, heat. It was these inbound stimuli that she was first aware of. And, as time passed, she began to make some sense of them, voices, shadows, movements.

So it was that three months and twenty-seven sols after the explosion in the soil processing cave, Dr. Jann Malbec opened her eyes and looked up at the world.

Over the next few sols Jann opened her eyes more and more. Each time, her understanding of what she was experiencing deepened. Across her field of vision shapes moved, blurred and indistinct. Sounds. *Were they voices? Saying what?* Finally, after around a week, she recognized a shape. It was a face, it was Nills, and the face said, "Jann, can you hear me?"

She tried to reply, but her brain had difficulty in establishing the correct procedure. So she simply blinked.

"I think she's come back to us," the voice said.

JANN'S MIND swam in a sea of dissonance, sometimes ethereal and dreamlike, sometimes reconnecting with the exterior world. At its most focused she could respond, just a word or two at first, *yes, no*. These lucid moments became more frequent, and over time she began to reconnect with reality. It was during this latter period that she began to have questions, lots of questions about why she and Gizmo were in the soil processing cave. These thoughts grew, with ever increasing urgency in her mind until her eyes snapped open. For the first time in what felt like an eternity, she felt truly awake and hyper-aware, like all the switches in her brain flicked on—all at once.

IT WAS MORNING. She wasn't sure how she knew this, but somehow she did. Jann instinctively tried to sit up in bed. Her body felt like clay and she was not certain of the position or location of her limbs. Her extremities seemed slow to respond to the signals her brain was sending. There was an urgency welling up inside her, forcing her body to respond. She swiveled her torso and slid her legs over the side of the bed. Then with one herculean effort, she slapped her feet on the floor.

Dr. Foster came rushing in, followed by Nills, then Anika. *How did they know she was awake and moving?*

"Holy crap, she's moving." Dr. Foster stopped dead in her tracks before rushing over to her again when she realized Jann was trying to stand.

"Jann, wait up, you need to take it slow." Dr. Foster grabbed her under one arm. "Nills, grab her other arm, will you? Help her back up on the bed."

Jann tried to fight them off. "I need to... stop them."

"Stop who. Jann?" Dr. Foster's voice was soft and patient, like a parent putting a child back to bed after a nightmare.

"VanHoff... Xaing Zu. I need to stop them, they can't leave, it would be disastrous."

"It's okay, Jann." Nills rowed in with the platitudes.

Jann stopped and looked at the doctor. "Who are you?"

"That's Doctor Foster. One of the AsterX crew. She's here to help you."

"AsterX... but?" Jann's question trailed off and her obvious confused state allowed Nills and Foster a window of opportunity to get her back in the bed. Finally she looked across at Nills. "What the hell is going on?"

Nills shifted and looked down at the floor, he began to scratch his chin.

"Tell me."

"Okay. What's the last thing you remember?"

Jann thought about this. Vague, fragmentary memories drifted up from deep within her subconscious, or were they dreams? "The soil processing cave... with Gizmo... and... and..." She shook her head slightly, trying to give shape to some deeper fragments. "VanHoff... and the others, they were leaving... I... I can't remember anything more." Her shoulders slumped. The strain of remembering extracting a physical toll.

Nills looked over at the doctor and Anika for a moment and then back at Jann. "You've been in a coma for over four months."

Jann remained silent as shock began to register on her face.

"There was an explosion in the cave. You were very badly injured, barely alive."

"Your recovery is remarkable. Under normal circumstances someone with your brain injury would be... well, a vegetable. It's extraordinary that you're sitting up talking to us." Dr. Foster circled the bed as she spoke.

"What happened to VanHoff... and Jing Tzu?"

Nills looked down again and gave a deep sigh. "I'm not sure if you're ready to hear all this."

"Tell me. What happened?"

Nills sighed again. Then sat down on a chair and started.

"WHAT I'M GOING to tell you are only some of the events, as they were explained to me. When the explosion took place in the cave, I was still unconscious on that very bed that you're in now. It was a few sols later that I finally came around. So I tell you some of this third-hand."

He sat forward in the seat. "It was the Chinese robot, Yutu, that detonated. It had a self-destruct mode, I believe. Gizmo. I'm afraid... was destroyed."

"Gizmo? No!" Jann was visibly shocked, as if she had taken a punch to the gut.

"Yes, I'm afraid so. Fortunately the cave contained the force of the blast and retained its integrity. You were found near the airlocks. Your body was smashed to a pulp. Broken bones, damage to internal organs, and severe brain damage." Nills shook his head a few times. "I honestly thought there was nothing left of you to put back together. But... well, here you are." He gestured to her with open hands.

"VanHoff and the remains of the Xaing Zu crew both

took off from the planet within a few hours of each other. COM evacuated their people from Colony Two, but the rest of their respective crews were stranded here."

"Did they get back to Earth?"

"Yes, I'm getting to that. Anyway, we sorted out the mess, purged the colony environment of the bacteria and brought the infected back to reality. But we almost had to abandon this place." He waved an arm around. "Too much damage to sustain a full environment. So we moved most people over to Colony Two. The stranded COM crew are over there. We kept the stranded Chinese here. One was a biologist, so we thought he might help with putting you back together, Jann."

"Was Earth alerted to what went on, I mean, did they know what COM and Xaing Zu were bringing back with them?"

"Oh, yes, yes. We were in constant communication with them. They knew all right."

"And?"

Nills scratched his chin again and sneaked a glance at the others. They were staying silent, preferring to let Nills break the news. "Well COM were first to return. You have to understand that VanHoff and the crew were the first humans ever to have traveled to Mars and returned. There was a media shit storm. On top of that, rumors began to spread that he had returned with the secret to immortality, you know how these things get blown out of proportion."

"But the Janus bacteria, they did purge the spacecraft environment before they landed?"

"Yes, but..."

"Don't tell me it got out?"

Nills said nothing, just looked over at Jann. "It got out."

It was Jann's turn to be silent and the realization sunk in.

"They think it was the rover. Its internal environment was not part of the COM craft's main systems. So they simply overlooked it. And that's where they think it started."

"What's the situation now?"

"Not good."

"Not good?"

"At first they had a strict quarantine in place, but... I don't know, someone opened something they shouldn't have. I don't know all the details because they tried to hush it up at first, not cause a panic. But after a few weeks it was infecting the local population around Cape Canaveral."

"No." Jann put her head in her hands and began to rock back and forth. "No, no, no."

"I think maybe that's enough for the moment, Nills." Dr. Foster was getting concerned. "Let me give you something to help you rest."

Jann jabbed an index finger in the doctor's direction. "Don't even think about it. I've been out of it for too long."

Nills stood up. "It's okay. She needs to hear this."

The doctor backed down with a shrug of her shoulders.

"What about the Chinese? Were they okay?"

Nills sat down again, this time on the edge of the bed beside her. "No, they didn't escape either." He shook his head again. "I'm not sure of the full story there. They're very secretive. But again a week or so after they landed people started to go crazy."

"Jesus Christ, this is a mess. What have I done, Nills, what have I done?"

"It wasn't you that created this thing, Jann."

"But it was me that released it."

"Well, I for one, am damn glad you did, otherwise I would still be a lab rat... at best. At worst I'd be dead. So don't beat yourself up over it. How many times have you tried to stop them?"

Jann rubbed her face with the back of her hand. "They just wouldn't stop, would they? Not until they screwed everything up." She shook her head and looked up at Nills. "So what's the situation now? Did they get it under control?"

"Eh... no. Not as such."

"What... tell me, what?"

"They knew how to kill it, you know, saturated oxygen at low pressure. That may be easy to do up here, inside a sealed environment. But on Earth... not so easy. No sooner had they brought the infected in and cured them, they would get reinfected as soon as they went outside.

It's in the open... can't stop it. All they can do is slow the spread. But eventually it will be everywhere."

"How long?"

"The World Health Organization just sent us their latest report." Dr. Foster finally had something to add. "The current infection sites are localized to the area around Florida in the US and Wenchang in southern China. But new outbreaks are happening in Europe, Russia and South America. These outbreaks will start to rise exponentially over time. They estimate the entire planet will be infected within six to eight months."

Jann looked at her and shook her head again. "Why did you leave me in this state for so long?"

"We had no choice. We had to get the brain swelling down, and that meant induced coma."

"But for so long..."

"Your physiology is... unusual. I'm not an anesthesiologist, I had to be sure you would get the best chance of healing before taking you out of it. My duty is to the patient."

"You should have done it sooner. Earth would not be in the dire situation that's unfolding now."

"Well, I don't see how that would have changed anything."

Jann looked over at her. "Using a saturated oxygen medium is one way to expunge the bacteria from the environment—but there's another way to kill it."

There was silence for a moment as they digested this new information.

"Another way?"

"Yes, Nills. What do you think I've been working on, holed up in my secret lab? I've been studying it, testing, probing. But mostly trying to find a way to control it. Ultimately I stumbled on another way to kill it without killing the patient in the process."

"We need to get this information back to Earth. This is great news." Dr. Foster was now visibly animated. "I need to tell the others." And she ran out of the medlab.

NILLS SAT on the edge of the bed and a craggy smile broke across his face. "I can't believe you're back—just like that. You are an extraordinary human, Jann." He reached in and gave her a hug. "You really don't give up, do you?"

Jann sighed. "It's this cursed bacteria, Nills. It's defined me. The life that I had has been wrenched from me because of it. It mutated my biology and gave me... superpowers, I suppose. But look what it's taken from me —from you, and all who live up here. Trapped us all in a never ending cycle of fear and conflict."

"It's gone from here now. We purged the colony. It doesn't exist anymore. Unless you have another secret stash somewhere."

"No, I don't. No more experimenting. We need to make sure it's gone from here forever. But even with that, we're back to where we started. COM and Xaing Zu may be gone, but there will be others. Don't you see, nothing changes?"

Nills shoulders slumped a bit. "That's a very pessimistic view, Jann."

"It's the truth, Nills." She reached and placed a weak hand on his arm. "You know it is."

Nills lowered his head a little. "They're not all like that. AsterX aren't interested in... genetics."

Jann sighed, "Oh Nills, you may be a technical genius, but you can be very naive sometimes. You trust people too much."

"Perhaps you're right, but then again, you can be a bit paranoid. No offense."

Jann laughed. "Yeah, but it's hard not to be when everyone is trying to kill you."

"Well they haven't managed to do that just yet, and the good news is you know how to kill this thing. Looks like you get to save the world—again."

"Maybe."

"What do you mean *maybe*?"

"I'm still... confused." She shifted in the bed, trying to move. "My body feels like lead."

"But you're cognizant... it's amazing."

"Yes, yes, a bit disoriented, that's all. Listen, Nills, before I do or say anything, we need a council meeting. And before that you need to tell me everything that's happened."

24

PANDEMIC

Nills wasted no time in bringing Jann up to speed on all that had happened, not just in the colony but also on the spread of the bacteria back on Earth. It was during his enthusiastic explanation of the intricacies of the asteroid mining exploits of AsterX that Jann began to lose focus. She was finding it increasingly difficult to keep track of the information. Perhaps it was merely a symptom of the dry subject matter, or more likely a manifestation of her own physical frailty. She could only keep her concentration for a relatively short period of time before losing track. She needed to rest. So Nills left her in peace, with strict instructions from Dr. Foster not to let anyone disturb her.

Now that Jann was left to her own thoughts she slowly began to realize that, ultimately, she had failed. All her efforts to protect Earth, her home, from the ravages of the Janus bacteria had come to nothing. It was now raging across the planet, doing exactly as she had predicted. Sending the people into panic. It was not just that it would turn one third of the population into homicidal psychotics, they in turn would probably kill at least another third. Whoever survived this holocaust would be living in a world devoid of utilities as industry and institutions ground to a halt. Law and order would break down for a while before any sort of equilibrium was reached—if at all.

But Nills was right. She didn't create this thing. This was the product of humanity playing god, of technology without bounds. And what were the colonists but guinea pigs for their creators' experiments? They had been used and grossly abused. *Goddammit, she shouldn't even be here.* If it wasn't for McAllister getting sick, well... she would be sitting happily back on Earth instead of trying to fight for the right of a handful of humans, on a far off planet, to live in peace.

She thought of home, of her father's farm. How she longed to walk the hills again, in the fresh clean air, with no need for EVA suits and life support. All the things the Earthlings took for granted. They didn't know how good they had it, always wanting to go one step beyond. How she would love to swim in a lake again, like when she was a kid. Those were happier times. How she missed them, the simple things: air, water, grass—and family. All gone now, no one left but her. Her father's ashes sat in an urn on some dusty shelf in the Green Mountain Crematorium, the funeral directors in the local town. She knew the son, Freddy Turlock, she went to college with him. *I wonder if he's still there, in the family business, or has he moved on, like me?* She laughed to herself at the thought of meeting him. *So what have you been up to, Jann?*

Oh, I've been up on Mars for a while. Trying to save a colony of clones from enslavement.

Really, and how did that go?

It was not right that his ashes be stored in some dusty drawer and forgotten, she would claim them and bring them back to the farm when she got home. That's what she would do. But, that was just a dream, a fantasy. She was here on Mars, no getting around that fact. If this place was going to be her home then she would make Earth respect it and its people. If all they wanted was to battle for control of Mars, well that wasn't going too well for them right now.

Jann could sense a window of opportunity opening in the midst of the carnage that now infected planet Earth. *Was it crazy for her to even contemplate this? But they might just be desperate enough to do it*, she thought. It's not hard to imagine what people will sacrifice to save themselves from the abyss. Time was of the essence. She needed to act quickly. And above all, what she needed to do was convince.

SHE AWOKE to find Xenon sitting beside her bed. His thin aquiline face broke into an elegant smile when he realized she was awake. "Jann, nice to have you back."

"Xenon, I thought... you were in Colony Two?"

"I was. But since you have requested a council meeting, and are in not any position to travel yet, we decided to come here."

"Oh... yes, meeting... that's right. Sorry... I'm still trying to get... my head together," she looked over at him. "Literally."

Nills arrived, followed by Dr. Foster. They must be monitoring her remotely, keeping an eye out for when she awoke. She sat up as the doctor fussed. Jann swung her legs off one side of the bed.

"No, you're not ready to move yet, you need to rest." Dr. Foster was trying to gently push Jann back in.

"I'm getting out of this bed, even if I fall flat on my face and have to crawl on the floor."

"Wait a minute," Nills stalled the protest. "I have an idea. Just stay there until I get back."

Jann decided to wait, but she still had her legs over the side. A minute or two later Nills returned—with a scrapyard wheelchair.

"I recognize that," said Jann. "Paolio's old chair."

"That's right, it still works. Come on I'll help you in."

By now Dr. Foster had conceded defeat, so she helped Nills guide the determined Jann onto the seat. Jann fiddled with the joystick, the wheelchair jumped back and forth as she gained a feel for it. Finally she looked up at Nills. "I'm starving. What's there to eat?"

Nills laughed. "Come on then, let's go find something."

Jann moved herself to the table in the common room, while Nills organized some food for her. It was only when she started to eat that Jann realized how hungry she was, it seemed she couldn't get the food in fast enough. Dr. Foster was also at the table, she looked on at this ravenous exhibition with a visible air of concern. Jann considered starting to cough and splutter and clutch her chest, just for a laugh, just to see how Dr. Foster would react. But, in the end she was too hungry to sidestep into amateur dramatics.

THE COUNCIL MEETING could not be held until all members had arrived. Xenon had already left in the rover to ferry across the remainder, which would take a few hours. Jann planned to use the intervening time to get a better understanding of the intentions of the asteroid mining company, AsterX, and its charismatic CEO, Lane Zebos. Her concern, apart from her natural state of distrusting anyone until proven otherwise, was the fact that Nills seemed to be besotted by them, particularly Zebos. They were thick as thieves, always talking, discussing, debating. Perhaps it was just a natural maternal instinct within her to feel a need to protect those she loved. Not to see them hurt by false promises and duplicity. After all, AsterX, like COM and Xaing Zu Industries were not here for the scenery.

She pushed the empty plate away, lifted up the coffee with both hands and sat back in the chair. She took a sip of the astringent brew, and raised it up towards Lane Zebos, who had been sitting quietly across from her. "Nice coffee, thanks for bringing it."

"No problem, it's Blue Mountain. I thought Nills would really like it."

"Indeed. So tell me, Lane. Why are you all here?"

There was a sudden silence around the common room, everyone stopped talking and readied themselves in anticipation of the bout that was about to take place. Jann Malbec was back, and she was now going to haul Lane Zebos and AsterX over the coals. No more mister nice guy, the free ride was over.

"Our mission is to salvage the Odyssey on behalf of the ISA." It was Lane's sidekick, Chuck Goldswater who answered. Lane raised a hand to silence him.

"That's just one element of it. The real reason we managed to get the governmental oversight we needed for this mission was to bring you back home."

"Well, that's very kind of you to come all this way just for me. But it looks like Mars is a much safer place to be right at this moment, what with Earth undergoing the zombie apocalypse."

"You said you knew how to kill it. We should get that information back as soon as possible, the longer we wait the more people will be affected." Dr. Foster saw her opportunity to push Jann.

Jann sipped her coffee. "So you're just helping the ISA out, is that it?"

"We're a mining company. Our business is the

extraction of physical resources for profit, it's very simple."

"So you want to mine on Mars?"

"No, not exactly." Lane leaned in and pointed vaguely skyward. "Out there, in the asteroid belt, lies the greatest untapped wealth in the solar system. We're an asteroid mining company, so our mission is to investigate whether Mars can be a waypoint for the exploration of the belt. Our objective is establishing a base on Ceres. From there we can investigate suitable asteroids for mining."

"So why cozy up to the ISA, surely they're no longer viable as a space exploration entity?"

"As far as they're concerned, you're still an ISA astronaut, on a mission." Chuck blurted.

Nills had joined the group around the table, but had remained silent until now. He burst out laughing. "Ha... you obviously haven't been reading the newspapers lately."

Lane gave his sidekick another look, to imply he should let him do the talking from now on. "Perhaps it was a naive dream to imagine that cooperation between international space agencies was the way forward for space exploration. That dream ended when COM landed the first settlers on Mars. I remember watching those landings. I was a kid then, it was what inspired me to pursue a career in space engineering. Even then I could see the future, and it belonged to corporations, not governments. But it is still a fallacy to assume that the privateer has it all their own way. There are laws governing what we do and how we do it, namely the Outer Space Treaty. And where there are laws there are politics. So in a sense, government still controls the exploration of the solar system. Those corporations who have the ear of government are those who will be the chosen few. Like a royal seal or a blessing from the Pope. It's almost medieval." He waved a dismissive hand. "It's very frustrating."

"So you needed to get into bed with the ISA so you could get oversight?"

"Correct. You see, AsterX are small fry. China is so powerful it can do whatever the hell it likes. COM too has become a monster, taking up a lot of political bandwidth. Their involvement with the ISA was the worst thing that the international space agencies could have done. It fractured them technologically. But they still have significant political clout, with tendrils leading right in to the heart of the UN itself. They can, and do, effect changes to the Outer Space Treaty."

"So the deal is you get to land on Mars and they get their spacecraft back?" said Jann.

"That, and they get to bring their astronaut home."

"And what makes you think I want to go back?"

Lane shrugged. "That's up to you."

Jann placed the now cold coffee back down on the table. She was a bit uncoordinated, it spilled when she set it down too hard. "I'm tired... I need to rest again." She moved the wheelchair back. "Nills, can you help me?"

Dr. Foster stood up to help as well. "I'm okay." Jann raised a hand to her. "Just Nills."

He lifted her into the bed in the medlab. "We should move you into an accommodation pod and out of here."

"It's fine for the moment." She was propped up with a multitude of pillows. "Do you trust this guy, Zebos?"

Nills sat down on the edge of the bed. "Insofar as I trust anyone. He is genuinely interested in exploring the asteroid belt. Deep down he's just an engineering nerd. I can relate to that. We've been talking a lot about it. How Mars could work as a waypoint." Jann's eyes closed. "Anyway, enough of my rambling. You need to rest before the council meeting."

Her eyes popped open again. "No, go on, I'm interested to hear it, don't stop."

"Well, we think we can build the craft here, on Mars. They would be robotic, initially. Simple enough engineering, although we would need specialist components from Earth. But it could be done in Colony Two. The one-third gravity here makes it considerably easier. Once a suitable asteroid is identified by one of the robotic scout missions, we send up harvester robots. The ore would be shipped back here for processing in Colony Two, we do a lot of that already. Then the final product would be shipped back to Earth."

"Do you think this is actually possible, I mean, in reality?"

"Absolutely, and it could be very lucrative."

"For AsterX."

"And for us. The main thing, though, is it would give us a future, Jann."

"Yes, I can see it would." Her eyes closed again.

"Jann, I'm sorry but I have to ask."

Her eyes opened again and her hand went to his. "Sure, what is it?"

"Are you really going to go back to Earth?"

She looked at him and squeezed his fingers. Her grip was weak. "I don't know, Nills. I can't say because I really don't know where home is anymore. Anyway, if the WHO is correct then there may not be an Earth to return to, at least not the same one I left."

"But you know how to kill this thing, don't you?"

"Yes, I do. But before I tell them, I want to know what's in it for us, for Mars."

25

ULTIMATUM

Jann emerged several hours later into the common room, now full of colonists. What constituted the governing body on Mars was now assembled. Nills, Xenon, Anika, Rachel, and several others that had been added to the council by merit of their knowledge. The only one that was missing was Gizmo. Not that the little robot was a council member but, it had always been a kind of counselor to Jann. Able to analyze a complex situation and present her with the decision forks and their respective consequences. She missed Gizmo, and felt a deep pang for its loss.

Also at the meeting were the crew of the AsterX mission, at Jann's request. No one was quite sure what was going down but the anticipation was palpable. When everyone was seated Xenon called the meeting to order.

He stood. "The colony council session will now commence." He paused. "The only item currently on the agenda is a general discussion of the epidemic that now afflicts Earth. I would ask Rachel to update us on the latest media analysis." He sat down.

"There's a very confused picture evolving. Rumor, counter-rumor, and conspiracy theories abound, reflecting a fragmented message being disseminated by the various governing authorities. Reading between the lines, I would say the situation regarding the spread of the infection is worse than anyone is admitting to. The general population is trending towards panic. I'm monitoring the intensity and frequency of several keywords and using these as a measure of general levels of anarchy. Best guess, I would say ten Earth days, maybe two weeks at most before the start of civil breakdown."

Chuck Goldswater jumped up. "This is crazy, if you know how to stop this pandemic then you must tell us now."

Lane grabbed him by the arm. "Sit down and keep quiet."

"But..."

"Now!"

Chuck sat down and folded his arms.

"Please forgive my associate's emotional outburst. It's a stressful time for all. Please continue."

Jann now took up the baton. "I think you are under the mistaken illusion that any of us here actually give a shit about Earth. Apart from myself and two others no one else has connections to Earth. And to you, they're all just clones." She looked Goldswater straight in the eye. "One could argue they are products of the machine, a machine whose only concern is the acquisition of ever greater wealth, and the self-aggrandizement of the egos that control it. What is happening on Earth, right now, is an unfortunate by-product. It is a self-inflicted wound, not of our making. Yet, by an ironic twist of fate it seems that the tables have turned and it is we who have the power of life and death on those who seek to enslave this place, these people—my people." Jann moved the wheelchair back from the table, and stood up, placing both her hands on the table for a moment as she established her balance. She stood up straight and scanned the council.

"That said, we're not monsters. We will not sit idly by and see Earth destroyed. That would be immoral." She directed this last word at Goldswater. "No, we will do what's right, but first there is something Earth can do for us. In two Earth days time there is a UN meeting in New York. Is this correct?" She directed her question at Lane.

"Yes, you're correct, two days."

"At that meeting I want them to declare Mars and the twin moons of Phobos and Deimos an independent, self-governing planet."

"Have you lost you mind? That's totally crazy!" Goldswater jumped up. He was apoplectic.

"Chuck, sit down, and don't open your mouth again."

"Bullshit, Lane. I can't listen to any more of this crap. It's clear her mind is gone, the brain damage is affecting her thinking."

"Chuck, if you don't stay quiet I will personally eject you. Now put a zip in it."

He reluctantly sat down.

"Much as I hate to say this, but the AsterX dude has a point, Jann," said Anika. "How do you suppose we get them to do that?"

"Thank you." Goldswater nodded at Anika.

"Hey, don't read too much into it, you're still an asshole," Anika hit back.

"Well, it's very simple, really. We withhold all information on how to kill the Janus bacteria until they do." There was a momentary silence around the room.

"Put yourself in their position," she continued, "...they don't really have any other choice." Jann lowered herself back on to the chair and moved it into the table.

By now the room was abuzz with astonished chatter. All except for Lane Zebos. He remained very quiet, staring intently at Jann.

"Okay, let's assume for a minute that *they*, whoever they are, were in agreement. An independent Mars in return for salvation. I still don't think you fully understand the sheer political complexity of obtaining such a resolution to the treaty. There would be a multitude of parties that might see this as an opportunity to stick it to the superpowers of the US and China. There would have to be unanimous agreement."

"No, there doesn't. You see, Lane, it was you who gave me the idea. And it's you that is going to fast track this for us."

"Ah..." A laugh escaped from him, unintentionally it seemed. "I don't mean to belittle your... proposal, but I think you have grossly overestimated the influence AsterX has in these matters."

"You're a partner with the International Space Agency. And, as you said so yourself, they may no longer be capable of getting people off the ground, but they still have political muscle. Through them we can go direct to the people who matter, the ones who can get this done, quick and painless."

Jann caught Nills' eye. A wry smile broke across the corner of his face.

"Jann's right. You've told me this yourself, many times," said Nills.

Lane argued, "It's just not that simple. I mean, the political and economic machinations of this proposal are labyrinthine. Not even a master analyst could fathom them." He stood up and started to pace. "Okay, let's say by some stroke of magic they agreed to this, and I can't see how they would, but let's say it actually happened. You give them whatever snake oil you've conjured up, they can just turn around and say, it wasn't you after all it was us, and the whole deal is null and void. I mean, there's no way on Earth, or Mars for that matter, that they will agree to this and then actually adhere to it. They'll say, yeah sure, and then find a way to renege at the very first opportunity."

"Yes, I know that. But it will still be law. And if it's law we can defend it. Not ideal but it means we have opened a new front."

Lane sat down again and looked at her.

"Look we're going to do this. You can help us if you want. If not, well, that's fine too, it's your decision. But just think about this for a moment. As a freely independent and self-governing planet, any requests to land on, even orbit, would require our approval. This, of course, would extend to mining rights. Particularly if Mars were to be used as a waypoint for the exploitation of the asteroid belt."

"Lane, you're not seriously going to consider this insanity?" said Goldswater.

Lane raised his hand again to silence his colleague. He stood up. "Let me see if I have this straight. You're offering us landing rights?"

"No, we're offering you *exclusive* rights. With those, AsterX would have a significant commercial advantage, a virtual monopoly on the wealth of the asteroid belt."

Jann could see a change in even Goldswater's body language. The sullenness was evaporating, his arms unfolded and he leaned in a little closer to the table. She had hit the mark.

"For how long?" he said.

"Long enough that it's in your interest to see the treaty is not overturned. There will need to be a review period of some kind, but ultimately our opportunity is now your opportunity."

"I'll agree, this is tempting, but what happens if you fail in this attempt to... blackmail Earth?" Lane rubbed his chin.

"Then mining the asteroid belt isn't going to matter, is it?"

There was a muted silence around the table as the implications of this sank in.

Finally, Dr. Foster spoke. "You're playing a very dangerous game. Billions of lives are at stake here, you seem to forget that."

Jann leaned in to the table. "Did we create this monster that is raging across the planet? No, Earth did. Did we start this war of worlds? No, Earth did. Did we seek to enslave the people of Earth? No, but they want to do that to us. You're right, Dr. Foster, this is a dangerous game. If you want to start a war, then you best be prepared for the consequences if you lose. We didn't start this, but we're sure as hell going to finish it."

Lane rose slowly from the table. "I need to confer with my colleagues for a moment, if I may."

Jann opened her hands. "By all means. But don't take too long."

It took only six minutes and forty-eight seconds, if any one was counting, for Lane Zebos and his crew to convince themselves that they had just been presented with the opportunity of the century. Complete and exclusive rights to the wealth of the asteroid belt. That was not to say that others couldn't go there. But it was as far, if not farther, away again from Mars, as the red planet was from Earth. A direct journey was an enormous undertaking. Without Mars as a waypoint, it would be commercially unviable for anyone. And, it would take several decades at least before technology would catch up enough to make the figures stack up for a direct mission from Earth. But by then AsterX would be so far advanced, it might not be possible to catch up with them. Perhaps they might even be established on Ceres.

IN THE COMMON ROOM, the colonists murmured and buzzed with a palpable excitement.

"My only concern," said Anika, "is that we are not going to end up like China giving Hong Kong to the British, or Macau to the Portuguese. We could be stuck with these guys."

"We'll need a review clause, and one that ensures production and processing takes place here," Nills chimed in.

Jann could tell from their body language when they returned AsterX were in.

"Okay, we'll help you, but there are no guarantees that we can pull this off. The main problems we see are twofold. One, we need a mechanism to verify the UN treaty is authentic. And secondly, how do we make it stick?"

"We may not have much clout in terms of political influence. But we can punch well above our weight on media spin. You need to remember that this colony was founded as a reality TV show. We've had our tendrils into Earthbound media for a very long time. We know how to spin a story, how to saturate the chatter, how to influence the masses. And, let's face it, this is one of the most powerful weapons there is. The ability to manipulate and influence.

This was Rachel's territory, so she immediately jumped in. "We would need a live TV broadcast from the UN chamber of the passing of the resolution. We will get this twenty minutes later. To verify that what we are seeing has not been tampered with we will re-broadcast back to Earth. It will then be picked up by our media associates and we can verify its authenticity."

"What can we do about making the treaty stick?" said Xenon, it was the first time he spoke during the session.

"Stories, Xenon. We need to disseminate the right stories. My gut instinct tells me we should herald this as a new opportunity for the Earthlings. Colonization is back on. *Come to Mars, free and equal, land of opportunity...* and all that. Make it like this treaty has made it possible for people to start a new life. That way any attempts to renege on it will be met with howls of protest."

"Very good, can you come work for us?" said Lane.

She laughed. "Well, it's just a first pass. We'll need

more themes and a multitude of variants, finessed for region, language, et cetera."

Jann looked over at Nills, he smiled back. As she scanned the others, she realized they were all on board. No going back now. It was game on.

26

UN

After the initial shock, the UN had wasted no time in calling an emergency meeting of the general council. And, as Lane Zebos had reasoned, their thinking was, *what did they have to lose?* They could go though the motions, concede to the demands of Mars, until they could ascertain if the colonists really did have a solution to control the pandemic. Then they could simply backtrack.

Since all of the five permanent members with a veto were affected, and fighting a losing battle to placate their respective populations, there was no problem getting their vote. Once they were secure, enough of the others fell into line to pass the resolution.

But its success was in no small part due to the work that the AsterX lobbyists did on the ground. It couldn't have happened without them. Yet, the colonists did not have it all their own way. Some argued that Mars was effectively a rogue nation, that they deliberately infected Earth, that they were being ruled by a maniac demi-god hell bent on the destruction of the planet. Others simply found the fact they had a gun put to their heads intolerable. But in the end, the resolution passed. Mars and its moons Phobos and Deimos were declared independent. However, there were some caveats. But for the colonists, it was enough. Perhaps not all that they had wished for but they had, at least, won the battle, if not quite the entire war. There would be more to fight for in future.

THE MOMENT they verified the authenticity of the UN broadcast Jann released a file, detailing how the bacteria could be annihilated, to seventy-four carefully selected media outlets, complete with notes on all her experiments and an extensive explanation of how to synthesize the active compound. She wanted the information in the public domain, not the preserve of some government agency or corporate entity that could control or profit from it. During the two days that preceded its release speculation was rife as to what information it would contain. When the denizens of Earth were finally put out of their misery, its revelations caused a shit storm of unprecedented proportions.

Was she totally crazy? was the primary response from the vast majority of Earth's population. Leaders were quick to call for the instant negation of the UN resolution that had just elevated Mars' status to one of an independent nation. Nevertheless, those who had been fighting to contain the pandemic: doctors, chemists and the myriad of scientists working in labs all across the planet, knew instantly that what Jann had discovered could, at least in theory, work. You just had to get past its perception in popular culture and simply look at the science.

JANN DESCRIBED how it was that she came to discover it in many of the interviews she did after the pandemic had been brought under control.

"I always wondered what was so special about the biology of Nills Langthorp. My mission, the ISA, that is, was decimated by this bacterial infection. Yet, first officer Annis Romanov, working as an agent for the Colony One Mars consortium, had been tasked with bringing back to Earth the biological analogue of Nills Langthorp—even in the midst of this mayhem. Why? What was so special?

"Remember, this analogue was a kind of living biological facsimile, used by the COM geneticists as a test bed for tinkering with the human genome, testing retro-bacteria... altering DNA. But it was free of the bacteria, and so was the real Nills Langthorp. All the rest of us, me included, had some level of it raging around in our physiology. How was that so?

I still had this analogue after the catastrophe of the ISA mission, but I did not possess the equipment to do any significant analysis on it. And, to be honest... I was a bit... preoccupied with being stranded alone, as I thought at the time, on Mars.

It was only after the discovery of the clone population in the mining outpost, and the upheavals that ensued, that I had the time and the resources to investigate it fully. We had extended the medlab in Colony One, and I had equipped a secret, subterranean sector with the necessary equipment. That's where I found the same Janus bacteria, still lurking in the soil processing facility. So now I had an isolated sample *and* the analogue. I could do my tests and try to get an understanding of its workings.

What came as a huge surprise to me was when I infected the biology of the analogue with the bacteria, it grew and multiplied just as in any other human. So there seemed to be nothing special about it. The only way I could control it, and kill it, was by pressure and oxygen. Then I would try again, and again, and again. But each time it was the same result.

Eventually I thought, *Maybe it wasn't Langthorp's analogue that was significant, maybe it was Nills himself. It was his biology.* That started me thinking about what environmental factors he had been exposed to—like low pressure, or saturated oxygen. I looked at his diet, what he ingested: plants, fish, the water he drank. Then it struck me. He was the only one of us to smoke a lot of weed.

There had to be some environmental factor that had

eliminated the bacterial infection in him. And certain cannabinoids were known to have antibiotic properties. Particularly the non-psychotropic ones. Some studies I remembered had shown positive results against the superbug MRSA. So, it seemed like a distinct possibility that this could be effective. At that time we still had some growing in the biodome so I harvested a batch and set about breaking it down into the various cannabinoid elements. The one I thought most promising, cannabigerol, turned out to be the most effective, eradicating all traces of the bacteria in the sample within twenty-four hours."

IN THE END, the efficacy of Jann's breakthrough prescription was verified in a very short period of time. Within seven Earth days of it being revealed, the pandemic had virtually stopped due to widespread availability of synthetic cannabinoids. It took only a further twenty-one days to fully eradicate it, such was the global effort applied to the task. This made Dr. Jann Malbec a figure of heroic stature in the eyes of many. Savior of the planet. Calls were made for the highest honors known to humankind to be bestowed upon her. But others didn't quite see her in such glowing terms. To some she was a diabolical and duplicitous schemer. A person to be vilified, not hero worshiped. There were also those who felt that Earth had just been conned out of its dominion of Mars, and, true to form, agitation commenced to have the UN resolution reversed. But as Jann had correctly assessed, possession was nine tenths of the law. And, once a treaty was enshrined in the statute books, it was damn hard to undo it.

THE ONLY CAVEAT, if you could call it that, was that a representative of the new government of Mars would be required to accept the resolution, in person, at the UN general assembly, before conclusion of the current session. That gave the colonists about five months.

They had considered simply using an AsterX board member as a representative. But Lane was not eager to be seen to be so involved. The optics of such a scenario did not look good, too much corporate involvement. So, after much discussion among the council it was unanimously agreed, Dr. Jann Malbec would go. She would take off from Mars onboard the AsterX MAV, rendezvous with the now salvaged ISA Odyssey orbiter, and return to Earth. Rachel particularly liked this touch as she could spin the story as Jann, the ISA astronaut, finally returning from her mission to Mars.

However, Nills did not take this news very well.

27

A NEW FLAG

The main entrance cavern in Colony Two was a hive of industrious activity. Groups of colonists were knotted around several large fabrication projects. Jann could make out a new flying bed being built, its skeletal frame rising up from the workshop floor. It was the first of two projects being fabricated for AsterX, the second being a robotic exploration craft. It would launch from Mars and head out to the asteroid belt. Jann was not sure of the technical details of the mission, but she could see it was taking shape. On the side of the small craft was emblazoned the newly designed Mars flag. It was not unlike the Japanese flag, a red disk on a white background. However, this had two smaller disks, one on either side of the main one. These represented Phobos and Deimos.

Some were concerned that it was too similar to Japan's national symbol. But Rachel argued that to gain

GERALD M. KILBY

acceptance people generally acted more favorably to what was familiar. It would be like it had always existed. It seemed to work, as the emblem now popped up everywhere. A number of colonists had already scratched the flag out on the surface of the crater. Large enough to be seen by hi-res satellite. Images of the colony were now flooding back to Earth to feed the insatiable interest in Mars, which had now reached fever pitch since the UN resolution.

These craft, the flying bed and the robotic explorer, represented the first physical manifestation of their success in gaining independence from Earth. Already a new AsterX mission was departing Earth orbit with scientists and engineers as well as specialist raw materials and components to support the fledgling space industry that was now developing in the colony. Negotiations were also well advanced for a new batch of colonists for the red planet. Things were going to get very busy around here.

One of the rovers had been brought inside the main entrance cavern and prepared for the relatively short journey to the AsterX MAV. They had decided here was the best place to say their goodbyes as more colonists could be present to witness it than out on the surface.

Jann was already encased in her EVA suit. Over her left breast the new emblem of Mars had been stitched, beside the ISA logo. Xenon walked alongside, carrying her helmet and gloves. Jann shook hands, nodded acknowledgments and accepted the multitude of personal goodbyes from individual colonists. Rachel walked beside her holding Jann's holo-tab. It contained, among other things, the text of the acceptance speech she was to give at the UN General Assembly. Rachel had rehearsed it with her, over and over, stressing the need to pause after certain statements, slow down or speed up her pace, all crafted to emphasize certain points. How Rachel knew all this Jann had no idea, but she was a natural born propagandist, as she jokingly liked to call herself. Jann's speech was a jumping off point for a barrage of finely tuned messages that Rachel and her team would unleash through their now extensive media networks. Rachel now had three other colonists working full time, doing nothing else but managing the message. Already the executives of AsterX were picking Rachel's brains as to how to do what she did. And to her great credit, she remained politely circumspect on her methodology.

In the background of all this was Xenon. His enigmatic personality left those who didn't know him wondering what the hell went on in his head. He seldom spoke, but when he did it was generally profound. He seemed to have an uncanny ability to know exactly what everybody was thinking and hence the best move to make. Rachel and he got along very well, she seemed to be the only one that Xenon would engage with in long conversations. So it came as no surprise to everyone when she proposed him for the title of President. No one objected, although some suggested Jann should also stand. But she declined. Her role, as she saw it, was as envoy. Nills also had no interest in such office, preferring instead to focus on the development of the colony as both a manufacturing hub for spacecraft venturing in to the belt, and as a processing plant for the refinement of returning ore. So the day-to-day management of the colony, was given to Nills and Anika. Xenon would be the face and voice of the colony, managed ever so precisely, by Rachel. There were others of course, but these were the first leaders on the now independent Mars.

As JANN APPROACHED the rover she could see Dr. Foster and Chuck Goldswater were both fully suited up and waiting for her. Lane Zebos stood beside them, talking. But he was not going. He had given his place to Jann, preferring instead to spend more time here on Mars working with Nills to see their dream brought to fruition. When he saw her he approached, crossing the distance in a few long strides.

"Ready to rock?"

"No. Where's Nills?"

Lane pointed across the cavern to a small workshop at the back. "Last I saw him he was in his workshop."

"Okay, give me a minute."

Lane nodded. "Sure."

Jann pushed her way through the crowd and over to where Nills spent most of his time these days. The door was open. She walked in. Nills looked up from his bench.

A filament of smoke corkscrewed up from a circuit board he was soldering.

"Oh Jann, sorry... I lost track of time."

Are you sure you're not trying to avoid me? she felt like saying, but resisted the temptation, it would serve no good purpose. They had been through all this, several times over the last few weeks, after it became clear that Jann was accepting Lane's offer to take his place and return to Earth. Nills of course knew why. His head understood the necessity for her to return, but his heart had a hard time accepting it. Not that it was any easier for Jann. She knew what awaited her on arrival, it would be challenging, to say the least. But she was thinking of the practicalities. Nills, on the other hand, was clearly deep in emotional territory, something he had difficulty managing. There was no set of plans for him to follow, no schematic to help him make sense of his feelings. This was new and he struggled with it. Already his mood had rippled through the rainbow of emotions associated with loss: grief, incredulity, anger and finally acceptance. So she forgave him for hiding out in here. Close enough to see her leave, but far enough away that he could handle it.

Jann looked down at an object on the workbench that Nills had been working on. She recognized it. "That looks like a part of Gizmo."

"It is. I've been working on him for a while... off and on... when I get the time."

"Him?"

"Ah… just doesn't feel right to call Gizmo an *it* anymore. I think he's earned the right to have a more personal pronoun… don't you think?"

"Do you think *he* can be rebuilt?"

"Yes, eventually. But, how much of the old Gizmo remains…" Nills gestured with a shrug, "…it's hard to know. His personality had been built up from countless interactions and experiences over a long time. I won't know until I finish how much is lost."

Jann picked up a charred component. It was a small square CPU, like a flat plastic millipede. Its outer surface coated with black soot, many of its pins were bent and broken.

"Is this from the old Gizmo?"

"Yeah, it's toast now."

"Can I have it, as a memento?"

"Of course."

There was a brief, awkward silence as neither knew quite what to say. "Are you ready to leave now?" was the best Nills could manage.

"Yes, they're waiting for me."

He stepped closer to her and held her arms. "I'm going to miss you around here."

She pulled him closer and hugged him tight. It was clumsy in a bulky EVA suit. They stayed like that for a moment until Jann pulled back her head. "Not too late to come with me."

"No, we've been over that. It's a bad idea. I'm a clone, remember. It would be a freak show back on Earth. No, this is your gig. I would serve no useful purpose." He smiled. "Anyway, who's going fix up Gizmo... and build all the machines that AsterX have ordered?"

"I know, Nills. But I had to ask, just one more time."

"Ahh... I'm sure the gravity on Earth would probably kill me anyway."

"Yeah, it's not something I'm looking forward to."

"You'd better go, don't want to miss your flight."

She was silent for a moment as she looked at him. "I have to do this, Nills. I have to go."

"I know." His voice was soft. "I always knew the sol would come when you would have to go home."

She lowered her head. "I'm not sure where *home* is anymore, Nills."

"Earth is your home, Jann."

"It *was* my home, now... I don't know."

She kissed him and broke away. "Remember me."

"You can count on it."

She walked out and tried not to look back. Jann kept her head down and pushed her way to the waiting rover. The rear airlock door was open. Dr. Foster and Goldswater were already inside. She stepped in and turned to wave back. A cheer went up. She sat down inside as the door was closed. The engine started and the rover lurched through the main entrance airlock and out onto the Martian surface.

Jann wept. No one spoke.

28

EARTH

Those on Earth that were infected and had survived would now have the same physical benefits that Jann and the colonists on Mars had, fast healing, longevity. They would presumably be the new elite. The bacteria had been eradicated but she had no doubt that samples had been saved and stored in labs all across the planet. How humanity would deal with the consequences of this event would be for historians to report. As of now, though, it was just speculation. Interestingly, those that had gone mad and were now free of the infection, gained none of its benefits apart from being simply normal. Of those that the bacteria had not driven insane, it had varying degrees of reaction. Some descended into the same depressive state that had affected some of the colonists, and became listless, even suicidal. But even those that had come out on top displayed varying degrees of biological alteration. Some healed quicker than others. These quirks of the infection had only become evident on Earth as the sample size was far greater than that of Mars. So now patterns could be seen.

Speculation abounded as to how this event could alter the course of human evolution. Was this the point where the genus of Homo sapiens forked and diverged, with a kind of new *super race* branching off from its root? Who could say? But there was no question that things would ever be the same again. It was estimated that, at its peak, over fourteen million people had been infected. A significant number, but still less than 0.2 percent of the global population. Of that number, a significant portion had been radically altered biologically, upward of four million, and another six million to a lesser degree. The big question now was, could this superhuman trait be passed on, could it be inherited?

THESE WERE NOT the questions that occupied Jann Malbec's mind as she sat in the back seat of a very large, black, bulletproof SUV. Ahead of her and behind her were similar vehicles, all packed with government security agents and support personnel. Overhead she could hear the ever present thut-thut of a chopper, waxing and waning as it circled overhead. In the front passenger seat an armed agent sat on high alert, eyes darting this way and that, sometimes talking into his cuff, sometimes pressing the discreet earpiece closer to his eardrum.

Sitting beside Jann, who was now referred to as the Martian Envoy by the various officials, dignitaries and press, was Ms. Teri Denton, a high-ranking AsterX executive, who had been assigned to look after her. In reality that meant fending off the hordes of press, media and lesser mortals who wanted a piece of her.

From the moment that Jann landed back down on Earth, Teri had been glued to her side like a growth. And even before Jann had spoken her first words to the ground crew, Teri was answering for her. From that moment on it was clear that a battle was starting. On one side was Teri Denton, on the other was pretty much the entire world of press, government officials, media institutions, scientists, advocacy groups, lobbyists, celebrity agents, brand managers, commercial interests, hawkers, hustlers, fans, fanatics and straightforward crazies. She fought them all off with the help of a backroom team of well groomed professional stonewallers. Nothing got through this perimeter defense system that didn't meet the exact criteria set by Teri.

Outside of this ring of steel were even more defense systems, radiating out in ever increasing circles. So, to gain access to the inner sanctum, one would have to pass through a series of tests, each one more intimidating than the previous. The prize, if one succeeded, was an audience with the Martian Envoy, Dr. Jann Malbec. Few managed this herculean feat. And Jann was very glad of that.

Such was the zeal that Teri exhibited in her role as guardian of this precious resource, that she was always on the alert—and ever present. So much so that Jann was pretty sure that, if not for the fact that it may be viewed the wrong way, Teri would have slept in the same bed as her.

However, her role also extended to making sure that Jann had whatever she wanted. And what Jann really, really wanted was to pay a visit to her old family farm in El Dorado County, California. So Teri had made it happen. Not an easy task considering it seemed to involve mobilizing a security team to rival that of the U.S. President.

She couldn't just fly there and rent a car like a normal citizen. Her fame had denied her that. Nor could she simply do what she wanted anymore. Every tiny detail of her life had somehow become seismic. What she ate, how she slept, where she went, what she watched, how she looked—particularly how she looked. Nothing was sacred, nothing was spared. She couldn't even stand and look out a window or her photograph would be on every media stream in less than five minutes. It was like living in a fishbowl. She had swapped one enclosed, encapsulated environment, that of Mars, for another, that of celebrity. And like Mars, moving outside the protection of the bubble could be perilous.

· · ·

THE SPEECH HAD GONE WELL. Crafted to touch on all that was necessary, hit all the correct points. It was like some ancient diplomatic acupuncture, it soothed the body politic, delivered with minimal pain and maximum effect.

But what most animated the world's media was not the substance of the address, nor the seismic event that this moment in the UN represented for humanity. No, what garnered the column inches and screen space was her dress. A flowing scarlet number, replete with full length cape, accentuating her form, highlighting her mystique and captivating all to the point of distraction— which was the whole purpose of it. It was brand Mars: conceived, contrived and designed by Rachel and her team, it was meant to convey a mystical, otherworldly aura, and it achieved it in spades. Particularly with the addition of a tiara that looked like it might be capable of receiving a direct transmission from Mars. But this was all optics, designed to give everyone something to talk about that wasn't substantive. It was like a TV talent show, UN style. Nevertheless, how she looked mattered more than simply creating a distraction. After all Jann was now in her forties, yet looked like a fresh-faced twenty-five-year-old. She was the physical manifestation of the power of the bacteria to alter human biology

JANN GLANCED out the side window of the vehicle. They had been traveling for quite some time on a narrow two-lane blacktop, twisting and turning their way though the vineyards and ranches of El Dorado County. This stretch of road was cutting its way through a forest of pine. Every now and again the tree-line would abruptly end and the land would spread out in rolling hills planted with vines. All about was green and verdant and bursting with early spring life.

The agent in the passenger seat touched his earpiece, nodded to himself and swiveled his head around to Jann. "ETA in two minutes, ma'am."

"I hope it's not going to be another freak show." Jann directed her statement at Teri.

"Shouldn't be. It's not an official visit, all on the QT."

Jann looked out the side window again but this time she directed her gaze upward into the Northern California sky. "Assuming you're not counting the flotilla of news choppers that have been following us since the airport." She had counted four earlier on.

"Don't worry, they don't have permission to land. We'll get you inside quickly."

"You know, if I open my mouth wide enough I'm sure the lenses they have could look right down my throat and see what I had for breakfast." Jann took her head away from the window.

"We're here," said the agent.

They slowed down and turned off the road in through an arched gate. Above it, a sign read *Green Mountain Crematorium*. The driveway was long, and swept through a manicured landscape that would put the Augusta National Golf Club to shame. Up ahead, a row of low brick buildings came into view. The driveway opened out into a parking area. It was empty of vehicles, presumably cleared out by order of the security team. The motorcade moved up to the front entrance and came to a halt under the large canopy that protruded from the front of the building.

Jann could see several people standing at the doorway, immaculately dressed, hands clasped in front of them, waiting to be introduced. She sighed, "Here we go again."

But before she could exit, the security piled out of the ancillary vehicles and took up predetermined positions, holding their earpieces, talking into their cuffs. Only when they were all happy could Jann, otherwise known as *the package*, be extricated from the vehicle and escorted into the building.

Jann stepped out and was immediately beset by the funeral director and his wife, an elderly couple in their late seventies. She shook hands and nodded as they exchanged formalities. However, the last member of the welcoming committee she recognized. He was a good deal younger, in his early forties, short in stature with a strange scarlet birthmark extending from his left earlobe all the way down his neck, and under his chin to his Adam's apple. He made no attempt to cover it up, at least not anymore.

"Hello, Freddy. You're looking well," said Jann.

He shook her hand and smiled. "Not as good as you.

You look just the same as the last time we met. You haven't changed a bit."

Jann laughed. "Looks can be deceptive, Freddy."

He gave a lopsided grin and he leaned in a bit closer to her. "I've been saying that very same thing to people for years." His voice was soft, as if what he was saying was meant for her ears only. He stepped back and extended his hand towards the interior of the building. "Come, this way, everything has been prepared."

They walked in through the front door into a wide, marble floored atrium, its tinted glass roof casting a kaleidoscope of colored light around the space. They moved to a large private office off the atrium. It was thickly carpeted with a wide oak desk dominating the central position. Around it were spaced several comfortable chairs. It was where the rituals of death were discussed as options in taste and affordability.

Sitting in the center of the desk was a modest urn. It contained all that remained of Dr. Jann Malbec's father.

Mr. Turlock took up his position behind the desk and placed a hand on the urn. "As requested we have extracted your father from his... resting place in the mausoleum."

Jann looked at him for a moment. "Thank you. You've been very kind. If you don't mind, though, I would like to conduct this business with just Freddy—for old times' sake."

Mr. Turlock looked crestfallen. He looked over at his son and like a fallen warrior passing the baton to his heir, he deflated and smiled. "Of course." He stepped out from behind the desk.

Jann swung around to the retinue of handlers and security agents. "Alone, if you don't mind."

Security staff talked into cuffs and Teri's face reconfigured itself into a look of utter rejection. She was being cast adrift from her charge. Her *reason for being* no longer wanted her around, albeit for just a few minutes.

"Certainly," she answered. "By all means, take as much time as you want." They were ushered out the door leaving Jann and Freddy alone. There was a moment's silence. "Drink?" said Freddy

"Really? You have alcohol here?"

"It's not against the law. And, well... a lot of people who come and sit in here, really need a stiff drink. It helps to get them through it."

"Yes, I see what you mean. What have you got?"

He opened the door to a cabinet concealed behind the desk and lifted out a half empty bottle of Chivas Regal and two glasses. "Whiskey okay?"

"Perfect."

He poured two glasses and then produced a tray of ice, from a freezer underneath the desk. Jann dropped two ice cubes in her drink as Freddy sat in the chair opposite her. They raised their glasses and clinked. Jann sipped her drink, sat back and looked directly at Freddy. "I'm trying to remember the last time we saw each other. It was graduation day, I think."

"Yeah. Long time ago now."

Jann looked around the room. "So you never did anything with your college degree?"

"I worked for a while as an intern for a lab up in Seattle. But, my father got ill so I came back to look after the business. I ended up staying, even after he recovered." He gave a sort of shrug. "I know it seems a bit odd. Being a funeral director is not generally a career path for a biologist."

There was a silence for a moment as Jann cast her mind back to a simpler time, when exams were the only stress. She had never paid him much notice until their final year when they started to gravitate toward one another. He, like her, was a bit awkward, self-conscious of his birthmark. He kept to himself and had few friends. But, it was during some college get together that they struck up a conversation and realized they were from the same neck of the woods, and knew a lot of the same people. One thing led to another and Jann found herself waking up beside him the next morning. In the end, nothing really came of it and they went their separate ways.

Freddy nodded at the urn that stood on the desk between them. "So what's the plan?"

"Take him back up to the farm and sprinkle the ashes into the stream that runs through the property. It irrigates the vines, so he gets to be part of what he created." Jann touched the side of the urn. "It was his wish."

"Have you been back there yet?"

"Not yet. It's hard for me to do anything these days, without a major mobilization of troops."

"It's in a bad way. I took a trip up there a while ago, just to see. Everything is either overgrown, running wild or dried out to a parchment. I'm afraid the house has been broken into a few times. But Sheriff Morton informs me it's just souvenir hunters, nothing too serious."

They didn't speak for a few moments and Jann realized that he was used to sitting here with people who needed a moment to compose themselves. So he kept silent as Jann thought about what she was going to do. She had been putting this off for a while, but her father had made this request in his will, so she felt duty bound to fulfill it.

"Would you come up there with me, now, today?"

Freddy thought about this for a moment, and hesitated. Jann put her glass down on the desk and leaned in. "It would be nice to have someone with me who..." she looked away and gazed out the window across the gardens. "Well... someone who I actually know." She looked back at him. "Strange as it may seem, Freddy, but you are the closest thing I have to a personal friend on this entire planet."

He looked at her for a moment considering this request. "Sure, I'd be honored."

"Just so you know, as soon as you step out there with me, your face will be all over the news feeds in five minutes."

He smiled. "You forget, I'm used to people staring at

me all the time." He turned his face and raised his chin to best display the birthmark down the side. "I'll make sure to present my good side."

"Thank you, Freddy. It's hard to do this on my own."

"No problem. Doesn't mean we're dating though."

Jann laughed. It was the first time she had done so since returning to Earth.

THE JOURNEY UP to the old vineyard was short, they were there in less than twenty-five minutes. Teri had been booted out of Jann's vehicle and Freddy installed in her place. As they traveled they pointed out places where people they knew had lived. Some were still there, but it seemed to Jann that almost everyone she had ever known here had either died or moved on.

The vineyard itself had formerly been part of a ranch that had been split up and sold off in lots. Her parents had come into some money and had had the romantically insane idea to move out of the hustle and bustle of the big city and engage in the agrarian lifestyle. But through a combination of naiveté, lack of knowledge and plain bad luck, that dream slowly faded into the harsh reality of subsistence fruit farming.

They turned off the main road through the gates to the property, and up the long drive to the house. Jann could see the effects of years of neglect. The plantings were parched and many were dead from lack of water. The olive trees seemed to have fared best and they were substantially bigger than Jann remembered. Already there were several security personnel dotted around. Presumably an advance party to check the place out before allowing Jann to set foot in such an open and unprotected space. Overhead she could hear the choppers circle around.

The SUV crunched its way across the gravel driveway and came to a halt in front of the house. Through the journey here she had rested the urn beside her on the back seat, cradling it with one arm. Now that they had stopped she brought it up and placed it in her lap and held it with both hands. The door was opened for her by a young and efficient security agent who stood back, motionless, one hand on the door handle, eyes darting this way and that as he waited for her to alight.

She turned to Freddy. "This..." she nodded at the urn, "...I have to do on my own."

Freddy nodded back. "I understand."

She stepped out into the afternoon sun, and made her way around the side of the house, through a small wooded area and down to the edge of the river that bordered the property. It was by far the best part of the place, and the reason that her parents had fallen in love with it. They spent many happy days here, fishing and swimming, when the river was high enough. She kicked off her shoes and waded in to the center of the stream. It was cool and refreshing. She lifted the lid on the urn and sprinkled the ashes into the water. It had been her father's wish, a romantic to the end. Perhaps he had some notion that he would be washed downstream and find his way into the vines that filled this valley. Maybe next year, when the new season wine was being drunk, the vintners and oenophiles would sniff its notes, taste its flavors and declare it an excellent vintage.

She stood there for a while watching the ash pool and eddy and slowly drift off with the gentle currents of the stream. She looked up from the water and took one last look around the home she grew up in. She stepped out of the stream, grabbed her shoes and walked back up to the waiting cars.

FREDDY WAS STANDING OUTSIDE LOOKING around when she got back. He waved when he saw her and then looked at her intently, perhaps trying to gauge her state. Careful to not say the wrong thing to her at this emotional time.

She waved back. "Mission accomplished. My father now sleeps with the fishes."

She sensed Freddy was somewhat taken aback by the glibness of her statement. She smiled. "It's what he would have said. He had many faults but at least he could see the lighter side of life. It was probably what sustained him."

"I can see what he liked about this place." Freddy scanned the landscape again.

"I can see the attraction, tending the vines, pruning, harvesting. Bringing life out of the ground sure beats the hell out of putting the dead into it."

GERALD M. KILBY

He looked back at Jann. "Oh... sorry, I didn't mean any disrespect."

"None taken." It was now Jann's turn to take a more studied look around the fields. "Why don't you do it then, you know, get yourself a small plot, live the dream?"

"I would love to but... I don't have the money for it, and then there's the family business, commitments, duty. You know."

"Well then you can have this place." Jann spread her hands out.

Freddy looked at her and laughed. "I don't have the finances for anything like this."

"Freddy, I'm not selling it to you. I'm giving it to you."

He stood there in silence for a moment. Jann could see he was trying to figure out what her angle was, what trick she was playing on him.

"Freddy, I see the same thing in your eyes, that same look my father had. You would cherish this place, wouldn't you?"

Freddy was looking around again, but this time she could sense he was taking stock. Perhaps seeing what planting needed to be done, which areas could be expanded, how new irrigation could be set up. He was hooked. Then he shook his head. "It wouldn't feel right, Jann."

"I want you to have it, Freddy. It would make me happy, and my father, to know it was in good hands."

He just stood there speechless, for a few moments. "What about you? I mean this is your home."

Jann looked around again, slowly this time. "For a long time I thought of this place, this Earth, as my home. But now as I look around, all I see is what's not there anymore, what's gone. I now understand that home is not about place, it's about people. Coming here finally made me realize—my home is Mars."

THE END

YOU CAN FIND the next book in the series, Jezero City : Colony Four Mars, here.

ALSO BY GERALD M. KILBY

You can find the next book in the series, Jezero City : Colony Four Mars, on Amazon.

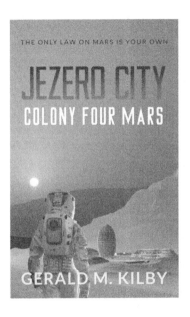

When a colonist dies in tragic circumstances, just a few sols before a major terraforming experiment, Dr. Jann Malbec begins to suspect that all is not what it seems.

ABOUT THE AUTHOR

Gerald M. Kilby grew up on a diet of Isaac Asimov, Arthur C. Clark, and Frank Herbert, which developed into a taste for Iain M. Banks and everything ever written by Neal Stephenson. Understandable then, that he should choose science fiction as his weapon of choice when entering the fray of storytelling.

REACTION is his first novel and is very much in the old-school techno-thriller style and you can get it free here. His latest books, **COLONY MARS** and **THE BELT,** are both best sellers, topping Amazon charts for Hard Science Fiction and Space Exploration.

He lives in the city of Dublin, Ireland, in the same neighborhood as Bram Stoker and can be sometimes seen tapping away on a laptop in the local cafe with his dog Loki.

Made in United States
Orlando, FL
19 September 2024